Robin Lewis

Robin Hood

LEGEND OF SHERWOOD

Robin Hood

LEGEND OF SHERWOOD

STEPHEN PERCY
LONDON, 1841

ADAPTED BY
Janet Stutts

EDITED BY
Robin R. Lewis

ILLUSTRATIONS BY
Greg Ruhl

HATHAWAY HOUSE, LTD.
FINE ILLUSTRATED BOOKS FOR CHILDREN
DALLAS, TEXAS
2015

Book design by Emily Hulen Thompson
Printed on acid-free paper in the United States of America

Library of Congress Control Number: 2015946116

ISBN 978-1-63016-304-4

Hathaway House, Ltd.
Dallas, Texas
www.hathawayhousebooks.com

Table of Contents

Merry it is in woods good and green,
when the thrush and blackbird sing.

I

BOYHOOD STORIES
NEAR THE SCHOOL PLAYGROUND

Early School Days

Tales of Robin Hood and his merry foresters were the delight of my boyhood. Many an hour, which my schoolfellows spent in games of cricket or leapfrog, I passed happily away in the rustic arbor that we had built in the corner of our playground, deeply intent upon a volume of old ballads that chance had thrown before me. Sometimes a companion or two, weary of the sport in which they had been engaged, would join me in my retreat and ask me to read aloud; and seldom would they leave me till the school bell warned us that it was time to return to our duties.

After the tasks of the day were finished, we had two hours at our disposal before we were again called to study our homework lessons for the following morning. In these short intervals we passed the happiest moments of our early days—forgetting for a while Caesar, Cicero, and Virgil, being freed from restraint, and exulting in our young lives.

Though many years have since glided away, I can recall these pleasures most vividly. Well do I recollect the youth who shared my home and who in school hours sat next to me in our sixth year when we were twelve years old; and well do I remember, as we sauntered together one bright summer's evening through the shrubbery that encircled our playground, his asking me to tell him some tale of Robin Hood. Willingly I complied.

There was an old sycamore tree close by, standing alone upon a little lawn. Its weather-beaten trunk was surrounded by a low seat, where, through an opening in the trees, a wide extent of country presented itself to the view. The shrubbery was upon the side of a steep hill, at whose base laid broad and verdant meadows. Through these, a navigable river wound peacefully along, bearing upon its surface the white sail of the pretty pleasure boat or the more dingy brown canvas of the heavily laden barge, constantly lending a fresh charm to the delightful landscape. Beyond the meadows was a little village, almost concealed by the venerable trees that surrounded it, while, to the left, the white front of some noble mansion glistened afar off, amid the dark tint of the distant foliage. Many a time had I chosen this favorite bench, and now, with my young friend at my side, I again reclined against the broad old trunk. Scarcely had we seated ourselves when another of our schoolfellows happened to pass by, and at the intercession of my companion, stayed to listen to my promised tale.

I endeavored to recall the earliest mention of my brave hero in the ballads that told of his exploits, and so I began to tell his tale.

Robin Hood's Youth

Very many years ago there dwelt within the green and shining glades of the northern part of England a most famous outlaw named Robin Hood, bold and sturdy in body and person. He lived during the reigns of King Henry the Second and his successor—his son, Richard Cœur de Lion, which is French for Richard the Lionheart.

Robin Hood's days on earth came when there were two groups of people living in the land. The Normans had come from France in 1066 with William the Conqueror—Duke of Normandy and grandfather of King Henry II—to fight the English. Though poor, these Normans were very proud and haughty. The Anglo-Saxons were the English whom the Normans defeated. In exchange for the Normans' military service, William paid them by stealing the Saxons' lands, houses, money, and cattle to give to the Normans. The Saxon nobles themselves often had to become the servants of these proud Normans. Even

Prince John, who ruled while his brother King Richard was fighting the Crusades, tried to please the powerful Normans, hoping they would make him King of England. Thus a very sad time began for the Saxons. Each of these peoples—Saxon and Norman—lived in England; each spoke their own language—English or French; and each hated the other.

The daring exploits and curious adventures of Robin Hood among the Normans and Saxons of England made him a renowned hero and have been celebrated in song throughout almost every country; and so great a favorite has he always been in England, that, as the old poet says:

> *In this our spacious isle, I think there is not one*
> *But he of Robin Hood has heard and also Little John;*
> *And to the end of time, the tales will ne'er be done*
> *Of Scarlet, George-a-Green, and Much, the miller's son;*
> *Of Tuck, the merry friar, which many a sermon made*
> *In praise of Robin Hood, his outlaws, and their trade.*

Robin Hood, whose true name appears to have been Robert Fitzooth, had not always been an outlaw; he had a good and proper upbringing. He was born and bred in the sweet town of Locksley, in merry Nottinghamshire, about the year of Christ 1160. He had been christened Robert, but Robin was the name by which he came to be called affectionately both by gentle and simple, such that his real name seemed likely to be forgotten altogether.

Robin had his father's sturdy build—muscular and tall of a height beyond the ordinary. Yet he had much of his mother's beauty; his bright eyes, frank and fearless, glanced and sparkled like stars. Though his mother died when he was young, she taught him to be true to his word, and his father, to be fair. His father's squires instructed him in the use of the sword; and some of the attendants trained him in handling the good old English weapons of the quarterstaff and the bow and arrows.

A very handsome youth, with light auburn hair, he was the most expert archer and the bravest wrestler among all the lads of the county, from whom he often bore away the prize in their rural sports. Occasionally wandering minstrels visited his home, and Robin would listen eagerly to the noble tales of King Arthur and his Knights of the Round Table. Best of all things in his life, however, was that he loved to wander in Sherwood Forest—the Royal Forest in Nottinghamshire—and to hear the whiz of the arrow as it cleft the air.

There was something of this lad that drew all hearts to him. Little Robin was well beloved by the people both of the castle and of the courtyard. He bore himself in the same fashion to high or low. He was as much interested in the poor laborers of cottage and hut as in the lords and ladies of high degree. He was fond of meeting people of every kind and condition, having much opportunity, since his father was an earl. Often had his generous heart been touched by the want and anguish of the poor; and he could see no reason, with such herds of deer filling the vast forests, why one of the King's subjects should suffer hunger, even though he knew that the penalty for slaying one of the King's deer was death. He knew that law well, for he had seen many sad instances of its enforcement among the poor.

Robin Hood and his family, all Saxons, had suffered at the hands of the Normans. In his young years, Norman King Henry the Second reigned. Later, Henry's son Richard became King. Though King Richard—a pious hero noted for his chivalry and courage—was revered by his subjects, including Robin, he left England to fight in the Crusades and was gone for most of his reign. In his absence, he gave the rule of England to two bishops whom he believed were good and wise. But his younger brother, Prince John, usurped the bishops' authority and ruled in his brother's absence, all the while intending to become the King himself. In the days of John's rule, justice did not abide in courts of law or in the officers of the Crown. Barons oppressed the poor, and the clergy did likewise; judges and sheriffs of the land used their high office only as a cloak for their corruption. He who had naught was ground down beneath the heel of him who had. Justice was scarce until it halted throughout the land; the King himself, far away, made not a single statute to protect the sturdy yeoman of good old England in their sovereign rights. Prince John tried to please the haughty Normans, for they were now great and powerful, and he hoped they would help to make him King of England, so he dealt dishonestly in all he did.

These were the days in which Robin Hood lived in the town of Nottingham of Nottinghamshire. His father, a Saxon noble, had not yet been robbed of land and money as many others had, but he had a bitter Norman enemy who at last came with soldiers, determined to destroy the earl and take all his goods and lands. The fierce and terrible fight ended with the killing of Robin's father and all his men. The Normans burned his house to the ground and stole all his money. But Robin, a young man by this time, escaped, for he was such a splendid archer that no soldier would go near him, either to take him prisoner or to kill him. In fact, there was no better archer in all the countryside. Tall, strong, and handsome, he nevertheless was gentle and tender, never hurting the weak nor scorning the poor, for it was his father who taught him to treat others with justice and to always be honest. Robin fought bravely till the last, but when he saw that his father was dead and his home in flames, he had not the heart to fight any longer.

Very fast he ran, for the Norman soldiers were close behind. Reaching the edge of Sherwood Forest he turned to see all the life he had known burning up in flames. He pressed on, plunging deeper and deeper under the shadow of the trees, hidden from any view of his father's enemy, who at last turned back. He threw himself down beneath a great oak, burying his face in the cool, green grass. His heart felt hot and bitter. Cruel men in one day had robbed him of everything. As he lay pressing his face against the smooth grass and clutching the soft, damp moss with his hands, the feelings of sorrow and pain were replaced with a longing to right the wrongs that changed his life.

The great, solemn trees waved gently overhead in the summer breeze; the setting sun sent shafts of golden light into the cool, blue shadows; birds sang their evening songs; deer rustled softly through the underwood; and bright-eyed squirrels leaped noiselessly from branch to branch. Everywhere there was calm and peace—everywhere except in poor Robin's angry heart; he was filled with righteous indignation. As images of his father's unjust death and the blazing fire that took his house flashed through his mind, flames of justice burned deeply in his heart.

In the dim evening light Robin removed his cap and knelt bareheaded on

the green grass to say his prayers. Then he stood up and swore an oath, saying:

I swear to honor God and the King,
To fight the cruel and help the weak,
To take from the corrupt to give to the poor,
So help me God, Your power I seek.

Then he lay down on the grass under the trees with his good longbow beside him and fell fast asleep. The next morning he determined to make these forests of Sherwood, which he loved from boyhood, his new home.

Robin Hood Earns Title of Outlaw

Not long afterwards, as Robin Hood was going to Nottingham, he passed by an ale-house, at the door of which stood several foresters—keepers of the King's parks—drinking ale and wine. Robin joined the party and entered into conversation with them when he learned that the King had commanded a shooting match to be held at a town close by in the course of the following week.

"I will be there," cried Robin Hood with great glee, "and will show King Henry a good arrow well shot with my longbow."

"Ha! ha!" laughed one of the foresters. "Do you think that a young one like you, as slender as a stripe, may shoot before a King? In faith, my young fellow, you must give place to better and more experienced men."

Robin Hood's brow flushed with anger at this slight, and he half drew his dagger from its sheath, but he recollected himself. "I'll wager you twenty crowns," he replied, "that I will strike a deer at five hundred yards."

"Done," cried the forester. "I bet you twenty crowns you cannot. Our host will hold the stakes while we go into the wood."

"Agreed," said Robin Hood, "and if I do not kill the deer you will win the bet." Each then paid twenty crowns to the host, and the whole party set out merrily to the wood. Young Robin strung his noble longbow, choosing one of his best arrows, and in a few minutes a deer bounded across the plain. Although the animal was at a considerable distance farther off than the space agreed upon, Robin would not lose the chance; he drew his arrow to the head

and let it fly with such force that when it struck the deer upon its side the poor creature fell plunging to the earth in a stream of its own blood.

"I'll take my money now," said Robin Hood proudly, to the host, as if it were a thousand pounds. "I've won the wager."

"The wager's none of yours," cried the man with whom he had laid the bet. "You had better take up your bow and be gone, or I will make you regret this day." And saying this he bestowed a light tap with his hand on the young archer's head, while the other keepers stood by and laughed.

Robin Hood knew that those in this group were not known for keeping their word and realized that they had no intention of giving him his just reward. It was an injustice that was typical of the likes of these men, even of the men in government who ruled by day and night. So he took up his bow as he was bidden, without saying a word, and ran away from them across the plain. When he had gotten some good distance off, he turned around, and aiming at the treacherous forester, let fly a shaft which struck through his cloak, pinning him to a tree. Before his companions had recovered from their surprise, Robin Hood sent arrow after arrow among them, causing a fear that moved them all to flee for their lives. Immobilized and shocked, the man hanging from the tree by a shaft through his cloak wrestled to escape, but Robin had just enough time to run back and grab the money owed him from the bet, which he stuffed in his shirt.

The people of Nottingham, hearing of this from the foresters who had escaped earlier, came out in great numbers to take the bold young archer in custody, but he had escaped far away before they arrived.

The Outlaws of Sherwood

Robin was young, but he was no coward. Sitting alone in the forest, upright, his chin propped in his hands, his brow knitted with thought, with bow lying beside him on the moss, he wondered what was best to do now that he was an outlaw—a wanted man.

Presently a cautious rustling sound in a clump of trees nearby startled him. His hand instinctively clutched at his bow. He sprang upright, feeling for an arrow. A man's head appeared from among the bushes, and then a tall fellow came from the trees toward him. Smiling, he stretched out his hands to show that he held no weapon. Robin lowered his bow as the man said in a gruff but kind voice, "Fear not, young sir! I do not seek your harm but your good! Will you listen to what I think you would find it well to hear?"

Robin lowered his guard and sat down. The stranger sat, and leaning forward, said in a low whisper, "News travels fast in the forest. Fear not! I know why you are here."

Robin listened closely as he continued, "It is no shame to kill what should be shared by all, for those who prohibit it stand for tyranny. I have come to you, lad, as a messenger from some good comrades who invite you to become one of them, one of us. They are all men who have suffered from the cruel use of power and injustice, even as you; men who like you are liable to punishment if captured and who for various causes have been outlawed like you. We live here in the forest, and we have often seen you, although you have not seen us."

Robin thought he was alone in the forest, but the stranger beckoned him to follow him. When he told Robin his name was Will Stutely, Robin thought he had heard of him before. As they walked, Will told Robin his story.

Will's mother was a widow, and her farm was confiscated by their lord, the Bishop of Hereford, because it happened to lie on the edge of his lands and he wanted more lands. Will stood up against the Lord Bishop's men and slew three of them, defending his mother's farm; so he was forced to flee. He told Robin, "My mother later died of fear and grief. I came here to the forest and met those whom you shall shortly meet."

Soon Robin and Will smelled the appetizing aroma of broiling venison and came into an open glade with a fire roaring in the midst, around which sat or stood roughly a score of men. Seeing Robin they gave a shout of joy and cried, "Welcome Robin, welcome to Sherwood!"

They led Robin to a rudely set table on the greensward and served the venison with plenty of good bread and ale. After the fire died down, the men sat or lay about on the mossy ground and told Robin why they had Will bring him to this meeting. One after another told the story of why he was now an outlaw; and in no case was the reason one of terrible crime or awful sin. They were tales of brave attempts to resist oppression from proud churchmen or haughty knights—of valiant rising against injustice in law and man. Robin's generous young heart, always kindly and quick to protect the poor and downtrodden, burned hot within him as he listened. He resolved that he would give the rest of his life to avenge their wrongs and those of others like them.

After a time, Will spoke. "You see, lad, what we are—outlaws, yet not truly criminal. We heard what happened to you, and since we need a leader, we thought you might fill that place for us, now that you are an outlaw too." The faces of kindly, weather-beaten men all turned toward Robin in trust and hope.

"Ay," he answered, "I will be your leader, young as I am. But hark ye, men!" And he sprang to his feet. "Remember, having been oppressed ourselves, we must aid those in like kind. Even more! These must be the laws that all in our band must follow. First, we will fight against all the Norman tyrants who are enriching themselves with spoils torn from the rightful owners of the soil, our Saxon brethren. We will regard the lowly against the proud, being bold with strength of soul. Second we will offer no violence to any poor or needy man, but will instead aid him with the wealth we may gain from Norman sheriff or baron or churchman. Seeing those who suffer wrong, we will defend and avenge him who is oppressed. Third, we will ensure that no lady, rich or poor, Norman or Saxon, shall have aught to fear from us. You must hold them all in high esteem for the sake of our mothers. These are the laws of our fellowship. Outlawed we are through misfortune, but criminal we must never be! If you consent to these conditions, I will do what you desire."

Then there arose a mighty shout and a celebration, which lasted well into the night. Justice, beaten out with clubs from courts and churches and castles, dwelt in the stout hearts of Robin Hood and his bold men of Sherwood Forest—brave yeomen all, each driven from the common meeting places of men by the wrongdoings that befell them in the name of the law.

For a long time afterwards Robin Hood dared not show himself in any town or village, as a reward was offered for his apprehension; but he lived in the forests under the greenwood trees with his new companions, growing strong in the healthful outdoor life. His skill with the bow became greater than ever; and despite his youth, his men rendered him both obedience and love. His inborn personal charm attracted nearly everyone with whom he came in contact.

Life in the Greenwoods of Sherwood

In these times, immense tracts of land, especially in Nottinghamshire and Yorkshire, were covered with dense woods—royal forests governed by the Crown—which generally abounded in deer and every description of game. As these were the property of the King, rangers or foresters were appointed for their protection, and the penalty against anyone who dared to slay a stag was death.

Robin Hood and his companions cared very little for these rangers, who indeed stood but a poor chance against them. They shot the King's deer whenever they were in want of food and cooked it well enough by a fire kindled with branches of the royal trees.

They likewise were sometimes bold enough to stop his majesty's liege subjects upon the highway and politely request the loan of a few pounds, which was most frequently granted them without their giving any security for its repayment, the poor traveler being glad to escape with a safe body.

As the young outlaw continued to live in Sherwood Forest, his superior skill in archery and his prowess at all manly exercises gained him great fame. Many young men joined him in his retreat and placed themselves under his leadership, so that he soon found himself captain of between sixty and one hundred gallant youths. They all dressed themselves in woodland cloth and leather of Lincoln green jerkin and generally wore a scarlet cap upon their heads. Each man was armed with a dagger and a short basket-hilted sword and carried a longbow in his hand, while a quiver filled with arrows, hung at his back. The captain, besides wearing a better cloth than his men, always carried with him a bugle horn, whose notes he taught his followers to distinguish at a most incredible distance.

There in the greenwood they lived a merry and free life. They righted many a shortcoming in the workings of the lopsided tribunals of Nottinghamshire by maintaining in due and orderly fashion the superior law of the forest, which, being put into words was this: rich or poor, fair play for all, and honor to no velvet coat, but honor to him to whom honor is due—who hath a stout heart, true and merry; a keen eye; and a strong right arm.

The poor loved Robin and his men, for they held to the compact that Robin had proposed. Many a starving widow was provided with food, and many a poor, pretty maiden given a dowry—all taken from the coffers of some proud bishop or overbearing earl. The Church was corrupt in those days, as was often a priest or abbot unworthy of his sacred calling. But Robin distinguished between the Church and its officers. The good clergymen who realized their sacred duties and who lived lives of simple piety came to love Robin as much as did their people; for they realized that he meant nothing but kindness to those who deserved it.

Life in the greenwoods of Sherwood was full of adventure. Many a fat and lazy bishop or high-born lord, puffed up with riches wrung from the poor, was forced to stop and pay unwilling toll to that merry band, and his ill-gotten gains were doled out again to all who had need in the countryside. Thus the name of Robin Hood was to those who waxed fat on the fruits of other men's labors a name of terror, but in every humble and honest home through the whole shire a word of household blessing.

Lord High Sheriff of Nottingham

Now it chanced at this time that there dwelt in Nottingham the most inveterate, most obdurate, most stubborn enemy of Robin and his merry men—the right worshipful, right powerful, right proud and haughty Lord High Sheriff of Nottingham. Many a time had good Robin put a spoke in the Sheriff's wheel when he or his friends sought to fleece some innocent squire or yeoman of his goods under fair pretense of right and proper process of law, and many a merry prank had Robin and his men played on that same most worshipful Lord High Sheriff.

So the Sheriff vowed a vow, by this and that and all he held most dear, to catch bold Robin, have him put in chains and punished with such dire punishment as was meet for a thief and a robber. Yet in all Nottinghamshire could he find not a single man to serve his warrant of arrest on Robin. Too dearly the yeomen and husbandmen loved him. Even a certain good tinker who set forth to Sherwood Forest to obey the Sheriff's commandment had fallen, instead, for love of the greenwood and its chief, and he joined the band, alack, in place of serving his warrant! Because that most worshipful Lord High Sheriff had suffered much scorn and laughter of men, he therefore vowed a still more awful vow than to have bold Robin Hood yet in irons!

Robin Meets Little John

All through the winter Robin and his men had had a very dull time. Nearly all their fun and adventures happened with people traveling through the forest on horseback. But in winter, most people stayed at home. So it was rather a quiet time for Robin and his men. They lived in great caves during the winter and spent their time making stores of bows and arrows and mending their boots and clothes.

One day Robin Hood said to his men, "My brave fellows, here have we been fourteen long days without any kind of sport; I feel dull and restless. Stay here a while among the green leaves while I go forth in search of some adventure. If I want your assistance, three blasts on my bugle horn will tell you where I am." And bidding them adieu for the present, he shook hands with them, and with his trusty bow in his hand, set out on his expedition.

He soon reached the high road, where he thought he should most easily meet with something to do, and marched along boldly for a considerable way.

He wandered on for some time without meeting anyone. Presently he came to a wide but shallow brook that ran across the road, over which there was but one slender, shaky bridge that would only permit a single person to cross at a time. Just as Robin Hood set his foot upon the plank at one end, a great, tall traveler appeared upon the other side, and neither would return as they met in the middle of the bridge. The stranger was a tall handsome young fellow nearly seven feet high, the tallest man Robin had ever seen; but he was unarmed, except with a stout oak staff.

"Go back," cried he to Robin Hood, "or it will be the worse for you."

"Ha! ha!" laughed Robin, "Surely you jest, man. You go back."

The stranger laughed, and called out in reply, "I have as good a right to the bridge as you. You can go back till I get across."

Robin was so accustomed to being obeyed that he was very much astonished. He said, "Were I to bend this good bow of mine I could send an arrow your way before you could even strike." Between anger and astonishment he hardly knew what he did. And stepping back a pace or two he drew a shaft from his quiver and fixed it ready to shoot.

"You talk like a coward," replied the stranger, "with a longbow drawn against one who has but an oak staff."

"I am no coward," answered Robin Hood, "and that you will see. Stay on the bridge a while. I'll be with you again in the twinkling of an arrow." And laying aside his bow he ran back along the plank, plunged into a thicket of trees close at hand, and quickly returned bearing a good oak branch. While he was doing this, he looked at the stranger and saw that he was not only taller but much stronger than himself. However that did not frighten Robin in the least; he was no coward. The idea of a really good fight had made his temper fly, for, like King Richard the Lionheart, Robin Hood was rather fond of a fight.

"Now," with the stick in his hand, he cried to the traveler, "we are equally matched. Let's fight out our quarrel on the bridge. Whoever throws the other into the water will win the day, and so we will part."

"With all my heart," replied the stranger, "for go back I will not." And without a word further he bestowed such a thwack on the head of Robin Hood that his teeth chattered together.

"You will have as good as you give," cried Robin, and laid such a blow on the shoulder of his opponent that every bone in his body rung again. They then went in earnest and right good will, and thick and fast rattled the staves upon their heads and backs, appearing like men threshing corn.

> *The stranger gave Robin a knock on the crown,*
> *Which caused the blood to appear,*
> *Then Robin, enraged, more fiercely engaged,*
> *And followed with blows more severe.*
> *So thick and fast did he lay it on him,*
> *With a passionate fury and ire,*
> *At every stroke, he made him to smoke,*
> *As if he had been all on fire.*

Getting more enraged at every stroke, they laid about each other with such wild force that their jackets were flying as if in a dance. The stranger felt he could not stand it much longer. Gathering all his strength at last, he gave Robin Hood a mighty blow upon the side of his head that made him stagger; and losing his balance, the outlaw tumbled into the brook. The blow was so fierce that the stranger himself nearly fell in after him.

Robin disappeared under the water, and with astonishment, wondering where he could have vanished, the victorious stranger cried, "Where are you now, my fine fellow?" He thought he had drowned Robin, which he had not meant to do. All the same he could not help laughing, for Robin looked so funny as he tumbled into the water.

"Good faith," replied Robin Hood, "I'm in the water, floating bravely with the tide. But you are a bold man, I must say, and I'll fight no more with you. You have the day, and that's the end of our battle."

Then wading to the bank Robin caught hold of a projecting branch of a tree. As he pulled himself out of the brook, the traveler came to help him saying, "You are not an easy man to beat or to drown either," with a laugh and twinkle in his eye. "It is a long time since I have met anyone who could use a stick as you can."

Once on dry land Robin and the traveler shook hands like the best of friends and quite forgot their banging and battering. Robin set his bugle to his lips and blew three such loud and lusty blasts that the woods and valleys echoed and re-echoed them until they reached the ears of his merry bowmen. In a few minutes they all appeared dressed in their bright green coats and arranged themselves round Robin Hood, who was lying on the grass to rest his bruised limbs.

"Good master," cried one of them named Will Stutely, "what do you want with your merry men? Have you fallen into the brook?"

"No matter," replied their captain. "This traveler and I have had a famous fight, and he knocked me into the water."

"We'll duck him, we'll duck him," exclaimed the men, running up to the stranger and seizing him by the arms.

"Stop!" shouted Robin Hood. "He is a brave young fellow and must be one of us." Then, springing to his feet, he advanced towards him. "I beg you to forgive my men. No one will harm you, friend, now that they know you are my friend," he said. "I am Robin Hood, and these merry men are mine." The stranger was very much astonished when he heard that he had actually been fighting with bold Robin Hood, of whom he had heard so many tales. Then Robin gave him an invitation: "If you will join us you will have a coat of Lincoln green like theirs, a dagger, a good broadsword, and a bow and arrows, with which we will soon teach you to kill the fat, fallow deer."

"I should like nothing better; here's my hand on it," replied the stranger, striking his palm into that of the bold outlaw. "I'll serve you with my whole heart. My name is John Little, and you will find that I can do much and that I'll play my part with the best."

"John Little? Why he is seven feet tall if he is an inch! His name must be altered," said Will Stutely, starting a contagious laugh that spread through the men, the wind carrying the sound of it all the way to the villages. When composed he said, "I'll be his godfather, and we'll have a merry christening in the greenwood."

Two fat deer were presently shot, and a fresh barrel of humming strong ale

was pierced for the occasion. Robin Hood and his followers then stood in a ring, while Will Stutely, attended by seven of the tallest, dressed themselves in black garments that had once belonged to some unfortunate priests and prepared to baptize this pretty infant. They carried him into the middle of the ring, and pouring some buckets of water over his face, for fear a little sprinkling might not be enough, he was as wet as Robin had been after he fell into the river. The men roared with laughter, but Will Stutely in a very solemn tone began to speak.

> *This infant was called John Little, quoth he,*
> *Which name shall be changed anon.*
> *The words we'll transpose, so wherever he goes,*
> *His name shall be called Little John.*

A loud shout from the men made the forest ring again. When this ceremony was concluded and when Robin Hood had given his new attendant a coat of Lincoln green and a curiously carved longbow, they all sat down on the grass to a merry feast. Music succeeded, and their bold captain, in honor of his new guest, trolled forth the following song:

> *You're welcome, my lad, to the forests of green,*
> *Where the wild deer so merrily bounds,*
> *Where the foresters bold their revels hold,*
> *And their bugle horn cheerily sounds.*
>
> *You will be an archer, as well as the best,*
> *And range in the greenwood with us;*
> *Where we'll not want gold nor silver, behold,*
> *While bishops have aught in their purse.*
>
> *We live here like squires, or lords of renown,*
> *Without ever a foot of free land;*
> *We feast on good cheer, with wine, ale, and beer,*
> *And everything at our command.*

Then welcome, my lad, to the merry greenwood,
Where the wild deer so joyously bounds;
Where the foresters bold their revels hold,
And their bugle horn cheerily sounds.

Merrily and happily did they pass the evening, dancing round some old, huge, and stately bald cypress trees—the monarchs of the forest—and listening to the pleasing ditty of one of their companions. At last the sun went down, and the deep shades of the forest began to draw around them. Robin Hood drew forth his bugle, sounded a few notes, and in a minute or two the whole band dispersed in groups to their huts and caves.

From that day on, Little John always lived in the company of Robin with his band of merry men. The two became such very great friends, and Little John became next to Robin in command of the merry men.

And so ever after as long as he lived,
Although he was proper and tall,
Yet, nevertheless, the truth to express,
Still Little John they did him call.

The Butcher

Shortly after this merry making, Robin Hood was one morning sitting by the wayside, amusing himself with trimming his bow and arrows, when he spied a jolly butcher going to market with a basket of meat before him upon his horse.

"Good morning, my fine fellow," said Robin Hood as he passed by. "What do you have in that basket there?"

"What's that to you?" replied the butcher. "You will not buy it, I guarantee."

"Now, my good friend, be civil," returned the outlaw, rising from the grass and patting the man's horse upon the neck. "What value do you put upon this beast of yours and the basket altogether?"

"Well, if you mean to buy," answered the butcher, still doubting, "you will have the whole lot for four silver marks."

"Throw that greasy frock of yours into the bargain," said Robin, "and here's your money." At the same time he took some silver pieces from a leather pouch that hung from his girdle and handed them to the butcher. With great joy at having made so good a bargain, the man instantly dismounted, and giving his horse's reins to his new owner, he quickly stripped off his outer garment. The bold outlaw as quickly encased himself in it and, mounting the horse, took the basket from the butcher and galloped off to Nottingham.

When he reached the town, Robin Hood made his way to the place where the meat was sold; and having put up his horse at an inn, he uncovered his basket, spread forth his meat, and began to call out for customers. He knew very little and cared very little about the price that was usually paid for meat, and the ladies in the market quickly discovered that he gave about five times as much for a penny as any other butcher. Even the Mistress Sheriff came forth after hearing the news, anxious to share in the great bargains the new butcher was offering. His stall was soon surrounded, and his brethren in the trade were left without a customer. At first they could not imagine what could be the reason of so strange an occurrence; they were filled with both interest and suspicion. When one of them learned that the new butcher had actually sold a whole leg of pork for a shilling, a general council was held, and it was unanimously agreed that he must either be mad, or some prodigal son who had run away with his father's property, but they were all determined to learn something certain about him.

When the market was over, one of them stepped up to Robin Hood. "Come, brother," said he to him. "We are all of one trade; come and dine with us today."

"Willingly I will," replied the outlaw, "and a jolly dinner will we have. It is my first day among you, and by my word it will be a merry one." They were soon seated at the board, at the head of which presided the Sheriff of Nottingham, while the host sat at the other end.

They commenced a most fearful attack upon smoking flanks of beef and many a goodly haunch of venison. The jovial outlaw did his duty with the rest, and when at last the dishes were taken away, he cried, "Fill us with more wine! Let's be merry, my brethren, drink till you can drink no more. I'll pay the reckoning."

"This is a mad blade," said the Sheriff to his next neighbor. "We must find out who he is." He continued aloud, "Have you, friend," addressing Robin Hood, "any horned beasts to dispose of?"

"Ah, good Master Sheriff, that have I," answered Robin. "Some two or three hundred, and a hundred acres of as good free land too as you have ever seen."

"I want a few head of cattle," rejoined the former, "and if you will, I'll ride this day to look at yours."

"Fill me a pack of wine," cried Robin Hood. "Here's to a good bargain!" And tossing off a goblet of wine, he rose up, threw a handful of silver upon the table, and with the Sheriff left the astonished butchers to finish their wine and talk of their extraordinary comrade.

The Sheriff saddled his riding horse, and tying to his girdle a heavy bag of gold wherewith to pay for his purchase, he set out with Robin Hood to Sherwood Forest. Merry were the jokes and loud was the laughter of the bold outlaw as they trotted along the road, and the Sheriff thought that he had never met with so pleasant a companion. "Heaven preserve us," said he, "from a man they call Robin Hood, who often frequents these woods."

"Fear not, Master Sheriff," replied Robin, "I saw him in Nottingham town not two hours ago, and I'll warrant me he has not overtaken us."

"In Nottingham!" cried the Sheriff, with astonishment. "Why did you not tell me that before? I must go back and capture him."

"It will be a profitless errand for you," answered the outlaw. "Though I know Robin Hood as well as my own self, it was with difficulty I recognized him in his disguise." The Sheriff looked hard at his companion, as he claimed so intimate a knowledge with the outlawed forester, but said not a word, only spurring his horse on faster and keeping as far from his fellow traveler as the width of the road permitted.

Presently they arrived at the borders of the forest and, striking into a narrow road that led through it, reached an open lawn of some considerable extent. Just as they entered upon it, a whole herd of deer tripped gaily across the path.

"How do you like my horned beasts, Master Sheriff?" asked Robin Hood.

"They are fat and in good condition, are they not?"

"I must tell you, good fellow," returned the Sheriff, reining up his horse and feeling a caution and regret inside, "that I would rather be elsewhere than in your company."

Robin Hood replied by taking his bugle horn from his side and blowing three distinct blasts that made the woods echo and his companion's ears tingle with no small degree of apprehension.

"You are a tricky fellow," cried the Sheriff, "and have played me deceit. Take that for payment." And the terrified Sheriff drew his sword and struck fiercely at the outlaw, who, spurring his steed aside, dexterously avoided the blow. In a moment after, sixty or more foresters, with Little John at their head, burst from the thickets and surrounded the two horsemen.

"Welcome, good master;" said Little John to his captain. "What do you want with your merry men?"

"I have brought the Sheriff of Nottingham to dine with you today," replied Robin Hood. "Make good cheer and give him the best."

"Ay, make merry, that will we," returned the tall forester, "for I know he has gold to pay for it." And gently obliging the Sheriff to dismount, he unfastened the bag from the unfortunate man's girdle, and taking his cloak from his shoulders, he spread it upon the grass and emptied the gold upon it.

"Three hundred pounds will serve us for many a carouse," said Little John, when he had counted the money and replaced it in the bag. "And now, Master Sheriff," he continued, laughing, "would you like venison for your dinner? Have you any stomach for a smoked haunch?"

"Let me away," cried the Sheriff, running to his horse's side, "or you'll all regret this day."

Robin Hood sprang to his assistance, held the stirrup while he mounted, and politely wishing him a pleasant journey home, he said, "Commend me to your good wife, Master Sheriff! Tell her I will save another goodly piece of meat for her when again I go as a butcher to Nottingham!" The poor Sheriff, glad to escape sound in body, returned no answer; but striking spurs into his horse was soon out of sight. The merry foresters quickly repaired to their usual spot, and with many a bumper of ale or wine, drank to the health and prosperity of the liberal Sheriff of Nottingham.

The bold outlaws were afraid to show themselves for some time after this adventure and for several weeks retired to a distant forest, where their haunts were not so well known as in Sherwood.

Just as I had concluded and my young companions were making their various remarks upon the merry life of the bold outlaws, the deep tone of our school bell rang in our ears. Off we started like a herd of deer frightened at the notes of Robin Hood's bugle horn.

II

OUR SECOND MEETING
BENEATH THE SYCAMORE TREE

On the next afternoon, when I took my seat beneath the sycamore, I found that it was surrounded by no less than six of my schoolfellows, so popular had been the legends of Robin Hood with my hearers of the previous day. I was mightily pleased at this and with renewed confidence began the following tale.

The Merry Will Scarlet

Robin Hood was one morning rambling among the woods, when through the branches of the trees, he caught sight of a carefree young fellow walking thoughtlessly along and whistling merrily. The stranger was clothed in a silken doublet of beautiful scarlet, his hose were likewise of the same bright color, and his bright green cap was ornamented with a crimson feather. By his side hung a handsome broadsword, the hilt of which was studded with precious stones, and in his left hand he carried an elegantly carved bow, while a quiver of polished oak, inlaid with silver, was suspended by an ornamented leather belt at his back.

He emerged from the thicket upon a little plain on which the noonday sun was permitted to shine unobscured by the deep foliage that on all sides surrounded him. As he stepped into the light, the traveler's heart leapt with joy at the sight of a herd of deer grazing quietly at the other end of the verdant glade.

"The fattest among you," said he, loud enough for the outlaw to overhear him, "will serve my dinner today." And drawing an arrow from his quiver, he fixed it upon his bow and discharged the weapon with such keen velocity that the noblest animal among the herd fell dead at the distance of forty yards.

"Well shot! Well shot, my friend!" cried Robin Hood, advancing from his concealment. "Would you like to be a forester in this merry greenwood?"

"From where did you spring?" said the stranger, turning round sharply at the sound of a voice. "Go your own way, and I'll go mine."

"If you will accept the place," returned the outlaw, unheeding this angry reply, "I'll make you a bold yeoman and give you livery of mine."

"Livery!" cried the other. "By my word, if you do not take to your heels, I'll give you such a buffet as will make your ears ring for many a mile."

Robin Hood drew back a step and bent his ever-ready bow, and at the same time the stranger, quick as thought, drew another arrow from his quiver and pointed it at the outlaw.

"Hold! Hold!" cried the latter. "This is cowards' play. Take your sword, man, and let's fight it out under that tree."

"With all my heart," replied the traveler, "and by my faith I will not leave you till you do cry mercy." Then laying aside their bows, each drew his sword, and stepping beneath the shade of a broad old oak, began the combat in right good earnest. The bold outlaw, seizing an unguarded moment, laid a blow upon the shoulder of his opponent that made him wince again, but in retaliation, the stranger rushed furiously at Robin Hood and struck him so violently upon the head that the blood ran trickling down from many a hair.

"Mercy, good fellow, mercy," he cried, dropping his sword's point to the earth and leaning himself against the tree. "You have fairly beaten me. Tell me, who are you?"

"Ha! You alter your tone now," answered the victor with a laugh, "but, if you are a true man, you may stand my friend. Do you know where dwells a yeoman they call Robin Hood?"

"Why do you seek him?" inquired the outlaw.

"I am his sister's son," replied the youth. "I had the misfortune of slaying

my father's steward by accident in a quarrel and am forced to flee from home; so I search for Robin Hood."

"Your name?" asked Robin Hood anxiously.

"I was born and bred in Maxwell, and my name is Will Gamwell," replied the stranger.

"My brave boy, I think I can guide you to him, if the aching head you gave me will let me. You have no further to look than to me. I am Robin Hood, and I am your uncle!" exclaimed the outlaw, joyously clasping him in his arms with delight. "You should have told me your name before we shed each other's blood. Welcome, kinsman, to the greenwood!"

"Forgive me, forgive me!" cried the youth, bending on his knee, "and I'll serve you day and night."

"Give me your hand," replied Robin, grasping it in both of his saying, "You are a bold fellow, a true marksman, and a right valiant swordsman, as I know to my cost. Let us go seek my merry men." And with many a pleasant discourse the newly found relations pleasantly whiled away the time on their path to the meeting place of the outlaws. As they approached the spot, Robin Hood drew his bugle from his girdle and sounded a few short notes. Before the music had ceased Little John stood at his side.

"Is danger at hand, good master?" he said. "Where have you tarried so long? From what comes this blood?"

"I met with this youth," replied Robin Hood, "and full sore has he beaten me."

"Then I'll have a bout with him," cried the tall forester, "and see if he will beat me too," and with a staff in his hand he stepped before the stranger.

"No, no," said his captain, interfering, "that must not be. He is my own dear sister's son, and next to you will be my chief yeoman."

"In that case, welcome, my friend, to merry Sherwood," exclaimed Little John, shaking the newcomer by the hand. "We'll have a rare feast for you tonight. But by what name will we call you among our jovial comrades?"

"His name is Gamwell," replied Robin Hood, "but we had better rename him as we did you; he has donned a fine scarlet doublet, and Will Scarlet will be his name." Then again taking his bugle, he set it to his lips and winded it till the warbling echoes waked from every dale and hill.

More than a hundred tall yeomen, clad in Lincoln green waistcoat, soon attended this summons, bounding among the trees like so many playful deer. Will Scarlet, frightened at the sight of so many men, all armed with bows, cried to his uncle to fly from them and was himself starting off at his full speed, when Robin Hood caught him by the arm and, laughing heartily at his terror, bade him behold his future companions.

"What wants you, good master?" said Will Stutely, the leader of the band. "Your bugle sounded so shrill, we thought there had been work for us."

"The danger's over now," replied Robin Hood, "but welcome your new comrade. He is my own sister's son and has proven himself a gallant youth, for he has given me a famous beating."

The foresters set up a simultaneous shout, and each advancing in his turn took the hand of the delighted youth. The rest of the day was spent in feasting and sporting, until the departing rays of the sun warned them to their caves and arbor hideaways.

The Monk's Prayer and Robin Hood's Golden Treasure

There were many days in which the outlaws of Sherwood scarcely knew how to pass away their time. They often grew tired of their easy and careless life, and longed for an adventure where more active exertions would be required. Robin Hood, especially, could ill tolerate the monotony of a forester's life. He was ever bent upon some enterprise, either by himself alone or with the assistance of his followers; and rarely a week passed but that the bold captain threw a good store of gold into his treasury.

One day, he disguised himself in the dress of a friar. A long dark-colored gown completely covered his green doublet, and a large hood over his head nearly concealed his features. His waist was girt round with a white woolen rope, from which were suspended a string of beads and an ivory crucifix. Attired with a staff in his hand, he took the high road and trudged on merrily. The first persons he met were an honest husbandman, clad in tattered garments, carrying a chubby boy in his arms, and his wife, with an infant, following mournfully in his steps. Robin Hood stopped them, inquired the cause of their grief, and learned that their cottage had been burned down by a party of raiders and that they were then on their way to Nottingham where the poor man hoped to obtain employment.

The seeming priest, moved with compassion at their forlorn state, drew forth a broad piece of gold and gave it to the wanderers, who ever after blessed the day they met the generous friar. Robin Hood walked on nearly a mile farther without meeting a single traveler, when at last he espied two monks in black gowns coming towards him, riding upon mules.

"Bless you," said Robin Hood meekly, as they drew near him, "I pray you, holy brethren, have pity upon a poor wandering friar who has neither broken bread nor drunk of the cup this day."

"We are grieved, good brother," replied one of the monks, "we have not so much as a penny. Robbers met us on the way, who have stripped us of all our gold."

"I fear you tell not the truth," returned the friar. "Why did they leave you those beasts?"

"Now," cried the second monk, "you are an insolent fellow," and pushing on their mules, he and his companion galloped off. The outlaw laughed at their hurried decampment, and then starting off at his best speed, he soon overtook them. "Brethren," he cried, as one after the other he pulled them from their saddles, "since we have no money, let us pray for some," and falling on his knees he made the monks kneel down beside him. The old ballad says:

> *The priests did pray, with mournful cheer,*
> *Sometimes their hands did wring,*
> *Sometimes they wept and cried aloud,*
> *Whilst Robin did merrily sing.*

After some time was spent, the outlaw rose. "Now, my brethren," said he, "let us see what money has been sent us—we will all share alike," and putting his hand in his own pocket he pulled forth twenty pieces of gold and laid them on the grass. The monks fumbled a long time amid their garments but could find nothing.

"Let me search," cried the friar, "perchance you have not hit upon the right pocket." The monks reluctantly consented, and presently the outlaw drew forth two purses and counted out five hundred golden crowns.

> *"Here is a brave show," said Robin Hood,*
> *"Such store of gold to see;*
> *And you will each of you have a part*
> *'Cause you prayed so heartily."*

He then gave them back each fifty pieces, which the monks eagerly seized; and running to the side of their mules, they were about to ride off. "Wait!" cried the outlaw, "Two things you must swear: first, that you will never tell lies again; and second, that you will be charitable to the poor." The priests fell on their knees and gave the required promise to Robin Hood, and then

> *He set them on their beasts again,*
> *And away then they did ride;*
> *And he returned to the merry greenwood*
> *With great joy, mirth, and pride.*

One of my hearers stopped me and asked, "Can you remember the whole of any ballad? If you could, I should like very much to hear it."

"And so should I."—"And I."—"And I," cried two or three other voices.

"I fear there will be some parts that you will scarcely understand," I replied; "but as you wish it, you shall hear of 'Robin Hood and the Ranger, or True Friendship After a Fierce Fight.'"

> *When Phœbus had melted the "sickles" of ice,*
> *And likewise the mountains of snow,*
> *Bold Robin Hood he would ramble away,*
> *To frolic abroad with his bow.*
>
> *He left all his merry men waiting behind,*
> *Whilst through the green valleys he passed,*

Where he did behold a forester bold,
Who cried out, "Friend, whither so fast?"

"I am going," quoth Robin, "to kill a fat buck,
For me and my merry men all;
Besides, ere I go, I'll have a fat doe,
Or else it shall cost me a fall."

"You'd best have a care," said the forester then,
"For these are his Majesty's deer;
Before you shall shoot, the thing I'll dispute,
For I am head forester here."

"These thirteen long summers," quoth Robin, "I'm sure,
My arrows I here have let fly;
Where freely I range, methinks it is strange
You should have more power than I.

"This forest," quoth Robin, "I think is my own,
And so are the nimble deer too;
Therefore I declare and solemnly swear,
I'll not be affronted by you."

The forester, he had a long quarterstaff,
Likewise a broadsword by his side;
Without more ado, he presently drew,
Declaring the truth should be tried.

Bold Robin Hood had a sword of the best,
Thus, ere he could take any wrong,
His courage was flush; he'd venture a brush,
And he was at it before long.

The very first blow that the forester gave,
He made his broad weapon cry twang;

'Twas atop the head, he fell down for dead,
O that was a terrible bang!

But Robin, he soon recovered himself,
And bravely fell to it again;
The very next stroke their weapons they broke,
Yet never a man there was slain.

At quarterstaff then they resolved to play,
Because they would have the other bout;
And brave Robin Hood right valiantly stood,
Unwilling he was to give out.

Bold Robin, he gave him very hard blows,
The other returned them as fast;
At every stroke their jackets did smoke;
Three hours the combat did last.

At length in a rage the forester grew,
And cudgeled bold Robin so sore
That he could not stand, so shaking his hand,
He cried, "Let us freely give o'er.

"Thou art a brave fellow, I needs must confess;
I never knew any so good.
Thou are fitting to be a yeoman for me,
And range in the merry greenwood."

Robin Hood set his bugle horn to his mouth,
A blast then he merrily blows;
His yeomen did hear, and straight did appear
A hundred with trusty longbows.

Now Little John came at the head of them all,
Clothed in a rich mantle of green;

And likewise the rest were gloriously dressed,
A delicate sight to be seen!

"Lo! These are my yeomen," said bold Robin Hood,
"And thou shalt be one of the train,
A mantle and bow and quiver also,
I give them whom I entertain."

The forester willingly entered the list,
They were such a beautiful sight;
Then with a long bow they shot a fat doe,
And made a rich supper that night.

What singing and dancing was in the greenwood,
For joy of another new mate!
With might and delight they spent all the night
And lived at a plentiful rate.

Quoth he, "My brave yeomen, be true to your trust,
And then we may range the woods wide."
They all did declare and solemnly swear,
They would conquer or die by his side."

This ballad was highly approved of; and when, as usual, a few remarks had been made upon the valor of the champions, I resumed my tales, and told of Guy of Guisborne.

Guy of Gisborne

How delightful are the woods upon a summer's morn. The bright foliage of the trees now shines in its deepest verdure; the lawns and glades are clothed with luxuriant grass and sweet wild flowers, upon which the dewdrops glisten in the rising sun. The merry birds, sitting upon the tender branches, pour forth their morning lays, and the lark, now soaring high towards the blue expanse of heaven, makes hill and dale echo with her melodious carol—all telling of the goodness of their Creator and praising Him for his wondrous works. Thus thought Robin Hood as, on a bright morning in the pleasant month of June, he wandered amid the trees of Barnesdale.

He had been awakened earlier than usual from his slumbers by the loud and incessant singing of a golden thrush. He arose and rambled forth, enjoying the freshness of the morning breeze and the sweet music that was borne upon it. Many a hare darted across his path, and many a young fawn skipped playfully at his side and then bounded into the recesses of the forest. At another time the outlaw's keen arrow would have followed them, but now he smiled at their merry frolics, and charmed with the loveliness of the scene, he rested upon his bow and contemplated with heartfelt pleasure the tranquil beauty of the morn. He continued, absorbed in meditation, when suddenly a distant sound broke upon the stillness of the air.

The outlaw listened for a moment. "It is the tramp of horses," he whispered to himself, and stepping to a tree, quick as a thought, he climbed among its branches. Then he could plainly distinguish the glitter of spearheads and bright helmets, and scarcely had he secured himself from observation, when several horsemen, followed by a troop of soldiers, passed within a few yards of his hiding place. As the leader, Robin Hood at once recognized his old friend, the Sheriff of Nottingham, who he had no doubt had now come with his men to seek the traitorous butcher of Sherwood.

It was not till some time after this little band had gone by that the outlaw ventured to descend the tree, and striking into a narrow path, he endeavored to retrace his steps to the spot where his men were dwelling. On his way he was obliged to cross the high road, where a stranger arrested his steps.

"Have you seen the Sheriff of Nottingham in the forest?" he inquired.

"Ah, yes, my good fellow, and with a fine band at his tail," replied Robin Hood. "Are you seeking him?"

"Not him," returned the stranger, who was a bold yeoman, dressed in a coat of the untanned skin of some wild beast, and who carried a bow in his hand and a sword and dagger at his side. "I seek not the Sheriff, but him whom he seeks."

"And who may that be?" said the forester, at the same time forming a pretty

shrewd guess.

"A man they call Robin Hood," answered the stranger. "If you can show me where he is, this purse will be yours," and taking a well-filled leather bag from his girdle, he rattled the contents together.

"Come with me, my friend, and you will soon see Robin Hood," returned the outlaw. "But you have a brave bow; will you not try your skill with me in archery?" The stranger at once consented. Robin Hood with his dagger cut down the branch of a tree and, fixing it in the earth, suspended upon the top a little garland, which he entwined with the long grass. The archers took their station at the distance of three hundred yards, and the stranger drew the first bow. His arrow flew past the mark far too high. The outlaw next bent his weapon and shot within an inch or two of the stick. Again the yeoman attempted, and this time his shaft flew straight and passed through the garland. But Robin Hood stepped up boldly and, drawing his arrow to the very head, shot it with such vehemence that it clave the branch into two pieces and still flew onwards for some yards.

"Give me your hand," cried the stranger. "You are the bravest bowman I've seen for many a day, and your heart be as true as your aim; you are a better man than Robin Hood. What is your name?"

"First tell me yours," replied Robin, "and then by my word I will answer you."

"They call me Guy of Gisborne," rejoined the yeoman. "I'm one of the King's rangers and am sworn to take that outlawed traitor, Robin Hood. When I have seized the rogue, I have but to sound this horn, and my friend, the Sheriff, who is in the forest, will know that I have won the day, and the great reward is mine."

"He's no traitor, sir," returned the forester angrily, "and cares as much for you as for the beast whose skin you wear. I am that outlaw whom you seek. I am Robin Hood." And in a moment his drawn sword was in his hand.

"That's for you then," cried the yeoman, striking fiercely. "Five hundred pounds are set on your head, and if I get it not, I'll lose mine own, for my debt is great."

Robin Hood intercepted the intended blow and fought skillfully with his fiery and more athletic antagonist, who poured down an incessant shower of strokes upon him. Once the bold outlaw fell, but recovering himself sufficiently to place a foot upon the earth, he thrust his sword at the ranger. Drawing back to avoid it gave Robin Hood the chance to spring up, and with one sudden back-handed stroke, he felled Guy of Gisborne to the ground where he lay motionless, but breathing still. Robin immediately stripped off the hide from the man, upon whom he put his own green mantle; and then taking his opponent's bow and arrows and bugle horn, he darted off swiftly through the thicket to assist his men.

Meanwhile the Sheriff of Nottingham and his attendants had pushed their way through the woods to Barnesdale, where they had been informed the outlaw was lying.

The bold foresters, ever on the alert, heard the unusual sound of the tramp of armed men and, with their bugles, gave notice to each other of the danger. Little John had been in pursuit of a fat doe, which he was bringing home upon his shoulders, when the warning sounded upon his ears. Concealing his booty among the underwood, he bounded through the forest to the scene of danger, where he found that Will Stutely and many of his comrades were urging their utmost speed to escape from some of the Sheriff's men, and two bold foresters lay wounded upon the grass. Little John's wrath was kindled. Forgetful of the imprudence of the action, he drew his bow and let fly an arrow at the cause of this mischief, but the treacherous weapon broke in his hand, and the shaft flew wide of the Sheriff and only struck a tree.

Left almost defenseless by the loss of his bow, Little John could make but a poor resistance to the crowd of men who instantly surrounded him. By the Sheriff's order, he was bound hand and foot, and tied to a young oak, receiving at the same time a promise that as soon as more of his comrades were taken he should with them be hanged on the highest tree in Barnesdale. Just then a loud blast from a bugle rang through the wood.

"Here comes good Guy of Gisborne," said the Sheriff, "and by his blast I know that he has slain that bold knave, Robin Hood. Come hither, good Guy," he continued as the outlaw appeared, effectually concealed in the yeoman's clothing. "What reward do you have for me?"

"I must finish my work first, good master Sheriff," replied the disguised hero. "I've slain the master, and now I must take care of his servant, but not before he has confessed his sins."

"You are a pretty fellow truly to want a confession from him," replied the Sheriff, "but go, do as you wish, only be quick about it."

The outlaw stepped to the side of Little John, who had easily recognized his beloved master's voice, and pretended to listen attentively to what the poor captive might be saying, but drawing his dagger, he gently cut the cords that bound his comrade and gave him the bow and arrow that he had taken from Guy of Gisborne.

Robin Hood then placed his own bugle to his lips and sounded a peculiarly shrill blast that rang in the Sheriff's ears as a death knell, so well did he remember the sound. The two outlaws were quickly supported by a band of sixty foresters, who had collected together, and all drew their bows at once against the intruders. A dense flight of arrows fell upon them. Those who were not too badly wounded immediately set spurs to their horses, or took to their heels in the most abrupt confusion. One poor forester, Will Stutely, they bore off with them. Robin Hood and his men pursued, and it was not till they had gotten half way on the road back to Nottingham that the defeated Sheriff and his attendants drew rein to a slower pace.

The Rescue of Will Stutely

Robin Hood was sorely grieved when he learned that his bold follower had been carried off. Calling his men together, he made them swear that they would rescue their brave comrade or die in the attempt. Will Scarlet was dispatched at once to learn to what place he was taken; and hurrying with all speed to Nottingham, he found that the news of the terrible brawl and the Sheriff's precipitate flight had already caused a great sensation among the gossips of the town. From them he easily ascertained that the captive outlaw was imprisoned in the castle and that he was to be hanged on the following morning at sunrise. Scarlet flew back with this intelligence to Robin Hood, who communicated it to his men, and all again swore to bring Will Stutely safely back to Barnesdale or fearfully avenge his death.

Early on the morning after his capture, a line of the Sheriff's archers and spearmen, bowmen and axmen came pouring out of the town. Rank after rank they swept forward until the gallows, erected on the plain in front of the castle, surrounded by powerful force of armed men, their spearheads and drawn swords glittering in the rays of the newly risen sun.

Last of all came the unfortunate prisoner, his arms bound and a white hood on his head. This hood the hangman would pull over the prisoner's eyes before the rope was put round his neck. Around Will marched a band of the Sheriff's stoutest fellows, and the Sheriff, who attended in person at the execution of so notorious an outlaw, rode beside the group, which guarded the outlaw. Will cast his eyes anxiously around in the hope that rescue might be at hand, but he could perceive no signs of the presence of his comrades. Turning to the Sheriff, he spoke up gallantly saying, "Grant me one wish, I pray you. Never has one of Robin Hood's men been hanged like a bandit; let me not be the first. Give me my good sword in my hand, and we will settle the matter; I will then die as a brave man should."

But the Sheriff would not hear of granting Will Stutely so brave a death. "I've sworn to hang you on the highest gallows in Nottingham," replied the Sheriff, "and when I catch that still greater villain, Robin Hood, he shall dance by your side."

"You are a shameful coward!" cried Stutely in a rage. "A faint-hearted peasant slave! If ever you meet bold Robin Hood, you will have payment for the deed you are doing. He scorns and despises you and all your cowardly crew, who would as soon take King Henry prisoner as brave Robin Hood." And the forester laughed loudly in defiance.

At the Sheriffs command, the executioner seized Will by the arms and hurried him to the fatal tree. He was just about to affix the rope, when a tall yeoman leaped out of a little thicket of hazels near the gallows and burst through the guards with the utmost coolness.

"What, Will!" he said, "Are you going to take leave of this world bidding good-bye to all your friends? I have come to take leave of you, Will, before

you die," cried the intruder, "and, good master Sheriff, you must spare him for me a while." Will looked up with a gasp of delight. He could not fail to know that voice and to recognize the huge form. It was Little John!

"As I live," cried the Sheriff to his attendants, "that rascal's a rebel too and is one of Robin Hood's men! Seize him! Five pounds for his head, dead or alive."

But, in the surprise and confusion following the moment in which the giant burst through the ring of guards, Little John was quick to act; he cut the bonds that secured his comrade and, snatching a sword from one of the soldiers, gave it to him, shouting, "Fight, Will, defend yourself, man. Guard your head! Help is near. To the rescue! To the rescue!" And turning back to back, the two outlaws gallantly fended off the attacks of the whole throng of their assailants.

The Sheriff ordered his men, "Seize the great rogue! Seize him, better yet, slay him!"

It was one thing for the Sheriff to call upon the guard to slay Little John, but to do it was another matter. For the giant stood there, his buckler on one arm, his huge, gleaming sword waving above his head, his ruddy face lit with the joy of battle, ready to crush to earth any who should dare to venture within reach of that mighty broadsword.

Then arose a still wilder shout of surprise and a louder cry of dread, for a long, clear bugle note rang out, and a band of archers sprang from cover of the forest and rushed upon the force, which the Sheriff had gathered.

"Bows and axes, comrades!" shouted the foresters. "Have at them!"

"To the rescue!" roared a host of voices from a neighboring wood, and Robin Hood, with one hundred forty men, bounded across the green plain. A flight of arrows from their bows rattled upon the armor of the soldiers, and more than one stuck into the Sheriff's robe.

"Away, my men, away!" cried the Sheriff, flying to the castle for shelter. "It is Robin Hood himself!" And the knowledge that the outlaw would especially choose him for a mark added wings to the speed of the valiant Sheriff. His men, not reluctant to follow such an example, vied with each other in the race, so greatly to the amusement of the merry outlaws that they could not for laughter discharge an arrow in pursuit of them.

The onset of the outlaws was so fierce and unexpected that the Sheriff and his men were borne back into the very gates of the town. This advantage lay to the credit of the brave and wily Little John. He had made his venture alone into the midst of the enemy in order to draw their attention and give his comrades a chance of taking them unawares, and he had succeeded nobly. In the uproar of the combat he cut his way easily through the ranks of the enemy and rejoined his friends, with Will Stutely at his side.

Robin Hood had his eyes everywhere at once. No sooner did he see that the prisoner and Little John were safe than he sounded the order for retreat to the forest. He had gained his end and, like a prudent leader, thought it wise to draw back in time.

"I little thought, good master, to have seen your face again," said Will Stutely, "and to you, my bold comrade," he added, addressing Little John, "to you I owe my best thanks. Will Stutely will never forget your kindness."

"May we ever support each other in danger," said Robin Hood, loud enough for the whole band to hear him. "But, my brave yeomen, we must be away, or we will have the whole nest of hornets about our ears." And with many a laugh at the sudden flight of the Sheriff and the glorious rescue of one of their favorite companions, the bold foresters plunged again into the woods and returned to Barnesdale, where they celebrated the joyful occasion with feasting and music, till the stars glittering through the topmost branches of the trees warned them that the hour of rest was at hand.

The Beggar

For some long time after this last daring adventure, Robin Hood and his men were so hotly pressed by the Sheriff that it was with difficulty that they eluded the pursuit. Now concealing themselves in the recesses of a cavern in the thickest coverts of the forest, they were obliged almost daily to change their abode, until at last, tired of the incessant chase, the Sheriff disbanded his forces and returned to Nottingham.

When the outlaws were well assured of this, they quickly came back to their old meeting places in Barnesdale and Sherwood and pursued their usual course of life. One evening Robin Hood was roving through the woods, when he espied a sturdy-looking beggar, clad in an old patched cloak, come jogging along. In his hand he carried a thick oak staff, with which he assisted himself in walking, and round his neck a well-filled meal bag was suspended by a broad leather belt, while three steeple-crowned hats, placed within each other, sheltered his bald head from the rain and snow.

"Wait, good friend," said Robin Hood to him as they met, "you seem in haste tonight."

"I've far to go, yet," answered the beggar, still pushing onwards, "and should look foolish enough to get to my lodging house when all the supper's done."

"Ay! Ay!" said Robin Hood, walking by his side. "So long as you fill your own mouth, you care but little about mine. Lend me some money, my friend, till we meet again. I've not dined yet, and my credit at the tavern is but indifferent."

"If you fast till I give you money," replied the beggar, "you will eat nothing this year. You are a younger man than I am and ought to work." And the old fellow pushed on still more briskly.

"Now, truthfully, you are but a bad-mannered vagabond," cried the outlaw. "If you have but one farthing in your pouch, I will part company with you before I go. Off with your ragged cloak, and let's see what treasures it conceals, or I'll make a window in it with my good broad arrows."

"Do you think I care for wee bits of sticks like them?" said the beggar, laughing. "They're fit for nothing but skewers for a roasting pigeon." Robin Hood drew back a pace or two and fitted an arrow to his bowstring, but before he could let it fly, the beggar swung his staff round his head, and with one stroke splintered the bow and arrow into twenty pieces. The outlaw drew his sword and was about to repay this with interest, when a second blow from the old man's stick lighted upon his wrist, and so great was the pain it caused that his blade fell involuntarily from his grasp. Poor Robin Hood was now completely in the beggar's power.

He could not fight, he could not flee,
He knew not what to do;

The beggar, with his noble tree,
Laid vigorous slaps him to.

He paid good Robin back and side,
And baste him up and down;
With pikestaff in hand, he swung wide,
Till Robin could only frown.

"Stand up, man," cried the beggar jeeringly. "It is hardly bedtime yet. Count your money, man. Buy ale and wine with it, and give your friends a jovial carouse. How they'll laugh at the poor beggar."

Robin Hood answered not a word but lay still as a stone, his cheeks pale as ashes, and his eyes closed. The beggar gave him a parting thwack and, thinking that he had killed the saucy highwayman, went boldly on his way.

It fortunately happened that Will Scarlet and two of his comrades were soon after passing by and, seeing a man lying by the roadside, apparently dead, walked up to him. What was their consternation and grief when they beheld their beloved chief weltering in his blood? Will Scarlet bent upon one knee and raised his master's head upon the other. One forester ran to a brook that flowed close by and brought back his cap filled with water, which they sprinkled upon his face, and his companion drew from his pouch a little leather bottle, the contents of which speedily revived the unfortunate outlaw.

"Tell us, dear master," exclaimed Will Scarlet, "who has done this?"

Robin Hood sighed deeply. "I've roved in these woods for many years," he said, "but never have I been so hard beset as on this day. A beggar with an old patched cloak, for whom I would not have given a straw, has so basted my back with his pikestaff that it will be many a day before Robin Hood will lead his merry men again. See! See!" he added as he raised his head, "there goes the man, on yonder hill, with three hats upon his head. My friends, if you love your master, go and revenge this deed; bring him back to me and let me see with mine own eyes the punishment you'll give him."

"One of us will remain with you," replied Will. "You are ill at ease. The other two will quickly bring back that evil-minded scoundrel."

"Nay, nay," returned the discomfited outlaw, "truthfully you will have enough to do if he once gets sight of you, with that villainous staff of his. Go, all of you, seize him suddenly, bind him fast, and bring him here, that I may repay him for these hard blows that he has given me. Vengeance is due this rogue, and who better to help meet it than my faithful foresters. Such a scoundrel will pay for his deed and greed."

Will Scarlet and his two companions started off as fast as they could run, dashing onward through many a miry pool and over many a tiring hill, until they arrived at a part of the road that wound through the forest by a way at least a mile and a half nearer than the beaten path that the beggar had taken. There was a dense grove of trees in the bottom of a valley through which a little brook gently streamed, and the roadway ran close to it. The foresters, well acquainted with every acre of the ground which they so often traversed, took advantage of this grove and concealed themselves behind the well-covered branches. Filled with righteous anger and feeling confident of forthcoming revenge on behalf of their beloved comrade and chief, they hovered in patient waiting, anticipating the delivery of blows this villain so rightly deserved. Their lying in wait also gave them a rest that renewed their vigor after such a fast paced chase through rugged forest.

Meanwhile, the old beggar, rejoicing in the victory he had so lately obtained, walked sturdily on, as briskly as age and his weary limbs would allow him. He passed by the grove without the least suspicion of lurking danger but had proceeded only a step or two farther when his staff was violently seized by one of the foresters and a dagger was pointed to his breast, with threats of vengeance if he resisted.

"Oh! Spare my life," cried the beggar, at once relinquishing his hold, "and take away that ugly knife. What have I done to deserve this? I am but a poor beggar who has never wronged you or yours."

"You lying, false miser," replied Will, "you have well nigh slain the noblest man that ever trod the forest grass. Back will you go to him, and before the sun sinks down, your carcass will be dangling from the highest tree in Barnesdale."

The beggar was sorely frightened at this terrible threat. But no thought of justice for his own misdeeds came even close to his mind, such little regard he held for it, even though now he felt like a victim himself. He had lost his only weapon, and his aged limbs were but a poor match against three stout young men. He imagined his decrepit demise at the hands of the young and strong, yet still without remorse for his recent past. In these moments he began to despair and to give himself up as lost, when a clever thought struck him. "Brave gentlemen," he said, with the skill of an actor in voice and countenance, "why take you a poor man's blood? It will make you none the richer. If you will give me liberty and promise to do me no more harm, I have a hundred gold pounds in this meal bag that will be yours." The foresters whispered together and determined to get the money first, come afterwards what might.

Not thinking what Robin would do, nor thinking with the sense that would make one wonder in the first place why an old beggar man would even have possession of a hundred golden pounds, Will said, "Give us your money, and we'll let you go your way." The beggar unfastened the clasp of his belt and, taking it from his neck, spread the meal bag upon the grass, while the young men, anxious for the gold, bent over, eager to seize upon the expected prize. The old fellow pretended to search very diligently at the bottom of the bag and pulled out a peck or two of meal, which he piled into a heap; then watching his opportunity, he filled both hands full and threw it violently in the faces of the outlaws, who, blinded and astonished, began to rub their eyes most woefully. The beggar sprung up in a moment, seized his staff, and in a twinkling began to beat their backs and shoulders.

"I have soiled your coats with meal," he cried, "but I've a good pikestaff here that will soon beat them clean again," and before the youths could recover from their consternation, the old man plied his staff so manfully that his arm ached from the exertion, and he was obliged to stop for rest.

The young outlaws did not attempt to retaliate. Their proposed revenge had turned inward, and they were lost in their humiliating blindness, completely embarrassed and incapable of accomplishing their feat. Indeed they could not see where to strike, but trusting to their swiftness, scampered away even more briskly than they had come, and the beggar, laughing at the success of his wile,

plunged into the woods and made the best of his way from Barnesdale forest.

When Will Scarlet and his comrades presented themselves before Robin Hood, the bold outlaw, ill as he was, could not refrain from bursting into laughter at their sheepish appearance. They hung down their heads and still rubbed their eyes, while the meal on their coats made known the trick that had been played upon them.

"What have you done with the bold beggar?" inquired Robin Hood. "Surely three of you were a match for him."

Will Scarlet replied and told him of their first success and the old man's promise of money, but when he came to the meal and the drubbing they had received, Robin Hood laughed till his bruised limbs ached. Although he would fain have revenged himself upon his opponent, yet the cleverness of the trick so pleased his fancy that he swore that if ever he met the sturdy beggar again, he would, by fair means or foul, make him join his band in merry Barnesdale.

This tale was frequently interrupted with the loud laughter of my schoolfellow hearers, who all praised the dexterity of the old beggar man. We all agreed with Robin that the beggar's cleverness earned him a place in Robin's band. And it brought to a happy end our stories for the day.

III

THE THIRD AFTERNOON
UNDER THE OLD TREE

Upon the next time that we met together, I found my schoolfellows waiting for me under the old tree; and taking my usual seat, I immediately began.

The Outlaws' Sports

Many a bright meadow bedecked with daisies and buttercups stretches its verdant surface by the banks of the fair river Trent, and many a wood filled with merry birds lines its brink so closely that the pendent branches of the trees bathe themselves in its transparent waters.

It was upon the evening of a lovely day in spring, when every flower looked fresh and beautiful, and the early leaves of the forest shone in their brightest green tint, that a party of young men emerged upon one of these meadows from the surrounding woods. They began to amuse themselves in the athletic exercises in which our forefathers so much delighted. Some of the men stuck slight branches into the earth and, placing a pole transversely upon them, leaped over it at nearly their own height from the ground.

Presently a signal was given, and four or five of the young men bounded across the lawn with the speed of young stags, vying with each other in the first attainment of the solitary elm that graced the center of the meadow. High swelled the chest of the victor as, breathless and panting, he received the reward of his achievement, perhaps a new scarlet cap or a bright new girdle sash, and proud was he to know that the chief to whom he had sworn allegiance beheld and smiled approvingly on his success.

But now a more important contest began. One of the foresters stood forward and fixed up a target, the face of which was rudely painted in circles of various colors, a small white spot serving as a center. A line was drawn at the distance of five hundred paces from this mark, near which about twenty bowmen took their station. One after another each stepped up to it, bent his bow, and let fly an arrow with all the force he could command. Many shafts had flown far wide of the target, and some few had struck it near the side, when the turn arrived for a brightly dressed archer to make his trial. Walking deliberately to the line, he very carefully placed his arrow upon the bowstring, raised it till it was on a level with his ear, and instantly discharged it. The quivering shaft sank deeply within two inches of the white center.

"Bravely done, Will Scarlet," exclaimed a forester who stood apart from the rest, and who evidently controlled their activities. "You will soon become as good a bowman as ever trod the greenwood."

"I do my best, good master," replied Will to Robin Hood, who had taken advantage of the cool evening, in order to exercise his men. "But here is one whom I fear I scarcely equal." And a bold forester, who was known to his companions by the nickname of "Much, the Miller's Son," stood forward, and drew his bow. The nicely balanced arrow shot as swift as lightning through the air and pierced the very center of the target. A loud hooray followed this achievement, and Robin Hood himself shouted louder than the rest.

A moment later, all was hushed, for the tall forester—brave Little John— took the last turn, and his comrades, knowing well his dexterity, breathlessly awaited the result of the contest. After carefully selecting a well-feathered arrow, he stood erect as a young tree, drew back his bowstring with the strength of a giant, and suddenly let it slip. For a minute or two no one could tell where the arrow had gone; it was just possible to trace its flight as it whizzed through the air, but it was not to be seen on the target. Little John, smiling as he beheld the looks of surprise, ran swiftly across the intervening space and, to their astonishment, drew forth his shaft from out of that of the miller's, which it had struck, and split in two about half way down.

Robin Hood and his followers shouted with glee, and the victor, bending upon one knee, received from his master, as a reward for his prowess, a beautiful arrow of silver. "Truthfully," said the outlaw, as he gave it to him, "I would ride a hundred miles, any given day, to find an archer like you."

"You have no need to go so far," cried Will Scarlet, rather envious of the better success of his companions. "There's a friar in Fountains' Dale on duty at the gate who will bend a bow against him or you or against all your men."

"I'll neither eat nor drink till I find him," said the bold outlaw. "It is too late to seek him this evening, but before I breakfast tomorrow I'll see this valiant friar." And as he spoke he drew an arrow from his quiver and fixed it upon his bowstring.

A young hare had innocently trotted forth from the shelter of the woods and was making its way towards the brink of the river, when the noise of the foresters reached its ear. Startled at the sound, the creature turned its pretty head, gazed for a moment, and, frightened at the unaccustomed scene, bounded at full speed back towards the concealment of the forest. The outlaw's keen eye had followed its motions, and wishing to display the superiority of his skill, he let fly an arrow at the hare while in its swiftest flight. The poor hare immediately dropped, although the distance between it and the archer was, at the least, a quarter of a mile.

"Do you think the friar at the Abbey of Fountains' Dale will beat that?" asked Robin Hood as he slackened his bowstring.

"That will he," replied Will Scarlet. "He has killed many bucks at half a mile."

"I'll never draw bow again," returned the chief, "if a lazy friar once beats me in archery. What say you, my friends, will we find out this gallant priest?"

"Make him join us!" cried several voices.

"Tomorrow at earliest dawn be ready to attend me," said Robin Hood, and with Little John by his side, he left the meadow.

The foresters then parted into groups and strolled away, some to the banks of the stream, others to the darkening woods, while a few, not yet content as to their inferiority, sought again to try their speed against the victors.

Friar Tuck

Upon the next morning, before the sun had risen above the horizon, Robin Hood started from his couch and armed himself. He put on his helmet and breastplate and took up his good broadsword, his long tried buckler, and his trustiest bow; then placing his bugle horn to his lips, he played so loud a reveille that his men, frightened from their slumbers, seized their nearest weapons, as if an army had appeared against them. A few gentler notes made them remember the appointed time, and soon fifty bold youths attended the summons of their master. He bade them hasten to Fountains' Dale by the shortest path but on no account to show themselves till he had sounded three blasts upon his bugle. And with a light foot and merry heart, he sprang into his horse's saddle and set out to encounter the renowned friar.

This friar, whose fame was spread far and wide, had once been an apprentice and one of the brethren of Fountains' Abbey, but his irregular course of life and lawless pursuits had brought down upon him the wrath of the superior, and he had been expelled. Friar Tuck, so was he called, bore his disgrace boldly. He immediately retired to the forests and there built himself a rude hut of the large stones with which the country abounded, thatching it with branches of trees. There he lived in solitude, gaining from the country people, who frequently came to him for religious consolation, a character of the greatest sanctity. The friar took care to turn this to his advantage, and many were the presents of butter, milk, and sometimes of a more enlivening liquid, that he received. But these did not constitute his chief means of livelihood. Early in the morning the friar had more than once been seen with a good longbow in his hand and a quiver of arrows at his side, and a report had gone abroad that few could equal him in the use of this favorite weapon.

The friar was a tall burly man, at least six feet high, with a broad expanded chest and a muscular arm of which the sturdiest blacksmith might have been proud. He usually wore a dark mulberry colored cloak that reached nearly to his ankles, and girded it with a black woolen rope, the two ends of which hung down before him about half a yard in length.

On the morning upon which Robin Hood had determined to discover him, for some unaccountable reason the friar had put a steel cap upon his head and a corset upon his breast, and with his long oak staff in his hand had rambled to the margin of the fair River Skell, where he stood gazing steadfastly upon the waves as they rippled by. Presently he heard the sound of a horse's step, and turning, he beheld within a few feet of him an armed horseman. The stranger quickly dismounted and, fastening his steed by his bridle to the branch of a tree, advanced towards him. "Are you the Friar of Fountains' Abbey?" he asked, when each had regarded the other in silence for a short space.

"They that speak of me call me so," replied the priest. "Why do you seek me?"

"Carry me over this stream, you burly friar, and I will tell you," replied Robin Hood. The priest, without a word, offered his broad shoulders for Robin to bestride. Gathering his frock up to the waist, the friar plunged into the stream and trod through the deep waters right manfully, with a firm, even step, not saying a word until Robin was safely on the other side and had leaped off lightly upon the opposite bank.

"Now carry me back, you merry gallant," said the friar, "tis your turn." Uncertain whether to laugh or be angry, the outlaw's sense of fair play prevailed.

Stooping he said, "Mount your steed, good fellow!" Robin took the friar upon his shoulders and with great difficulty bore his weighty burden across. "Now by my word you are double the weight that I am," cried Robin Hood as the priest alighted, and I'll have two rides to your one." The friar did not answer but, taking up the merry forester again, bore him to the middle of the stream and, bending down, pitched him headlong into the water with a smile as wide as the stream.

"Choose, my fine fellow, whether you will sink or swim!" he said. "A morning bath will do your health good." Robin Hood scrambled to the bank, angry that he had been dunked. He fitted an arrow to his bow and let it fly just over the treacherous friar for a warning, but the wet had sodden both the bowstring and the feathers of the shaft, and it flew far wide. The priest, not wishing to stand a second trial, flourished his staff and approached Robin; he

knocked the bow from the grasp of the forester, who quickly drew his sword and retaliated against his vigorous opponent. The friar at this grew wrathful and gave a most terrible thwack upon the outlaw's head. Blow followed upon blow; now the thick oak staff beat down the less weighty but more deadly weapon, and again the sharp edge of the sword drank blood. They fought for more than an hour, and each began to weary of such warm work before breakfast.

"A favor, a favor," cried Robin Hood, retiring from the contest. "Give me leave to sound three blasts upon my bugle horn."

"Blow till your cheeks crack," returned the friar. "Do you think I fear a bugle blast?" The outlaw sounded the horn thrice, so loudly that the friar clapped his hands to his ears and beat a retreat for several yards. The signal was immediately returned, apparently from close at hand. In two minutes more a tall yeoman leaped from the adjacent wood and, followed by fifty young foresters with bows ready in their hands, ran to the side of their commander.

The friar turned rather pale. "Whose men are these?" asked the friar, greatly surprised at this sudden reinforcement.

"They're Robin Hood's bold foresters," said the outlaw, "and I am Robin Hood. Will you join our merry troop? You are the bravest friar that ever wore a monk's hood, and if you can let fly an arrow as well as you can wield a quarterstaff, you are a match for my boldest man. Be our chaplain, as a stouthearted friar like you would be well suited to our band."

"Let's have a contest," said Friar Tuck, unwilling to fight against such odds as were opposed to him. "If there's an archer here that can beat me at the longbow, I'll be your man. If I'm the best, swear that you will leave me free in mine own woods."

"Agreed!" cried the outlaw. "Stand forth, brave Little John; and for the credit of Robin Hood, choose your truest shaft."

"Never fear me," replied the tall forester, as he carelessly advanced. "Shoot on, my brave fellow, and at what mark you may choose, but let it be some five hundred feet or so from us."

"Do you see that bird?" asked the friar, pointing to a hawk that, with fluttering wings, hovered at a considerable height above a neighboring brake.

"I will kill it. If you can strike it again before it reaches the earth, I'll say you are a better man than Friar Tuck."

Drawing an arrow from his quiver, with apparent ease, he shot the ill-fated bird, which instantly fell to the earth, but not before a second shaft had transfixed its body. A young forester darted away and quickly returned with the prize; it appeared that the friar's arrow had pinioned the hawk's wings to its sides and that Little John's had pierced through from its breast to its back.

"Well done, my brave archers!" cried the outlaws' chief. "Many a bowman in merry England would give his best weapon to shoot like you. What says my gallant friar? Will he keep his promise?"

Seizing Robin's hand in a mighty grip, the priest replied, "Ay, by my word! What I have said, that will I do. But first I must return to my hut and possess myself of its valuable contents." Robin Hood offered to accompany him, and dismissing his followers, he and the friar by turns rode upon the horse.

I know not your name," said Robin to the friar as they passed along. "But you need not tell it, for we usually give new names to those who join us. Because you did tuck up your frock to bear me through the stream, you shall be known among us as Friar Tuck."

"So it shall be," replied the friar. And together they went, first to the hut and then to the green woods of Sherwood.

Allen-a-Dale and Christabel

Shortly after the accession of Friar Tuck to his company, Robin Hood was one morning roaming through the forest, when he beheld a young knight, very elegantly dressed in crimson silk with his head erect and walking with a light and blissful step over the green plain, singing a roundelay; his face was lighted up with gladness, and his heart seemed overflowing with joy.

On the very next morning Robin Hood again encountered the same young knight as before. All his finery was gone. He wore a russet suit, and his countenance was overspread with melancholy. He walked slowly, absorbed in meditation, and now and then broke out into exclamations of the keenest grief. The outlaw's heart was moved. "What can have caused this sudden change," he said to himself. "Perhaps I may relieve his sorrows." And emerging from the grove, he stood before the young man's path.

"What ails you, my friend?" he said to him, "when yesterday you were as merry as a lark, and today you are as if you were at a funeral."

"Why do you ask," said the youth, "if you cannot help me in my distress?"

"I have a hundred yeomen as good as ever drew bow in the greenwood," replied the outlaw, "that will do my bidding as I order." But Robin felt inclined to learn more of the young knight. He asked him to sit down and tell him why he was so sad. So with many a sigh the poor young man told his tale.

"My name is Allen-a-Dale," he said. "Seven years ago I fell in love with the fairest maiden upon whom the sun ever shone, Lady Christabel. She loved me too, and we were happy. But her father was very angry. I was too poor, and he said we were too young to marry. He promised, however, that if we would wait seven years and a day, we should then be married. The seven years are over, and yesterday should have been our wedding day. I went to claim my bride. But alas! The knight would scarce speak to me. He said his daughter was not for such a poor man as I. Tomorrow she is to be married to another. He is old and ugly, but he has a great deal of money. So I have lost my love, and my heart is broken." Then poor Allen-a-Dale dropped his head in his hands and groaned aloud.

"Nay, do not grieve so. A maiden who changes her mind like this is not worth so much sorrow," said Robin.

But Allen-a-Dale shook his head. "Alas!" he signed, "She loves me still. It is the old knight, her father, who forces her to do this thing. Lend me your aid," cried the young man eagerly, "I have no gold. But if you bring my true love back to me, I will serve you faithfully forever and a day. I cannot shoot so far or so straight as your good men, but I can make and sing sweet songs and play upon the harp."

Feeling the righteous indignation that so often swelled within him, and scheming to right this wrong, Robin inquired, "Where is the wedding to take place?"

"At Dale Abbey in the valley between here and Nottingham." replied the lover; "It is not five miles distant."

"We will see what is to be done," rejoined Robin. "Come with me, and by my word it shall be arduous, but you will get your fair maiden, young man!" Taking the now hopeful knight by the arm, the outlaw led him away.

Great preparations were made for the approaching wedding in the village church that Allen-a-Dale had mentioned. The Lord Bishop of Hereford was there, dressed in his gorgeous robes; and the cottagers, decked out in their holiday costume, were waiting anxiously to witness so grand a marriage. An old minstrel with a long flowing beard likewise demanded and received admission into the interior of the sacred edifice, claiming he heard there was to be a great wedding and that he had come to see it and make a song about it. He wore a somber-colored mantle that entirely covered him and carried, slung by a belt across his shoulders, a harp, which, as he seated himself near the altar, he placed at his feet, ready to strike the strings on the appearance of the bridal party. From this vantage point, the minstrel could hear conversations among the people who all sympathized with poor Christabel the bride, knowing that she loved another.

Soon the wedding guests began to arrive. There were a great many lovely ladies in beautiful dresses. They came in rustling in silk and laces, nodding and smiling to each other, fluttering and flitting about the aisles of the great, dimly-lit church like pretty painted butterflies. The minstrel watched them beckoning and whispering to each other. Sometimes he could hear what they said.

"Poor girl," said one, "so young and pretty."

"And he so old and ugly."

"Not to say wicked."

"And she loves someone else, I hear."

"Yes, Allen-a-Dale."

"What! the handsome young man who sings so beautifully?"

"Then why does he not carry her off?

"Oh, he is too poor."

"Oh, the pity of it!"

The minstrel, trying to learn as much as he could about the bride, was glad at what he heard, for he now knew that everyone in the church felt sorry for poor Christabel. His plan was taking shape.

Presently the grave old knight entered the church, older and uglier than can be described. Silence fell upon the church as he entered. Nothing was heard except the ring of his gold-headed cane on the flagstones, as he hobbled up the aisle. So old and ugly was he, older and uglier even than the minstrel had expected. He was decked out in a suit of white satin, which only made him look more aged and withered.

Suddenly there was a little stir at the great west door. All heads were turned. The bride had arrived. A sigh of admiration passed through the crowd. Young girls, dressed in white, scattered roses in the path as she advanced, and the harpist sounded his noble instrument. The poor maiden seemed totally unconscious of all that passed. With slow and stately steps she came, with her head bent to the earth as she leaned on her father's arm; and tears burst from her eyes, following each other down her lovely cheeks. Pale as any lily, she came robed in shimmering white satin. Round her white throat and in her golden hair, luminescent pearls gleamed in the dim light. If the bridegroom was more ugly than the minstrel had expected, the bride was far more beautiful. Behind her came the little choir boys, dressed in red and white, singing a melodious wedding song.

They reached the altar rails, and the old knight was unmoved by his bride's sadness. The Bishop opened his book and began the ceremony.

"I forbid this match," exclaimed a voice that seemed to proceed from where the harper sat. It was the minstrel.

The Bishop, surprised at so unusual an interruption, stopped and looked around. "Stand forth, whoever you are, and state your reasons," said he, after a long pause. "Who are you who thus disturbs the peace of our holy service?"

"This old knight is not the damsel's free choice," cried the old man, rising from his harpist seat, "and I forbid the marriage." The ladies screamed, and at once the whole church was in commotion.

"I am Robin Hood," said the minstrel, and at the same moment, pulling away his false beard and casting aside his cloak, Robin Hood drew a bugle horn from his sash and stunned the ears of Bishop, knight, and maiden with the

loudness of his blast. Everyone stopped screaming and pressed forward, trying to catch sight of the famous man of whom they had heard so much.

At his distinctive summons, four and twenty yeomen darted out of a grove that was close at hand, bounded like wild deer over the plain, and quickly entered the church. The first man among them was Allen-a-Dale, who rushed to the altar and hurled the old knight aside. Lady Christabel raised her eyes and saw that Allen-a-Dale was standing beside her. Her face was no longer pale as she put out her hand timidly and slipped it into his. She looked like a queen with head erect and shining, happy eyes.

"Now, my good Lord Bishop," said Robin Hood, "do your duty; marry this fair lady to her own true love."

"That cannot be," returned the Bishop, closing his book with a loud clap. "The law requires that the church announcements of the marriage be published three times in the church."

"We will soon remedy that," cried Friar Tuck, stepping forward from among the bowmen. "Good master Bishop, I will do that office myself." As he spoke, he entered the enclosed space by the altar and stood by the side of the Reverend Father, who, with a very ill will, suffered his robe to be taken from his person.

The foresters and villagers, one and all, could not restrain their mirth when the tall yeoman, Friar Tuck, put the Bishop's fine gown upon himself and took up the Bishop's volume. Everyone laughed as he stepped to the rails of the altar, he looked so fat and jolly. For fear that thrice might not be enough, he published the announcement seven times, while Allen-a-Dale and his betrothed took their places at the altar steps.

Then he began the marriage service. "Who gives away this maid?" asked Friar Tuck when he had finished that part of his duty.

"That do I," answered Robin Hood, who stood at the damsel's side. "Where's the man who dares dispute my gift?" and clapping the bridegroom upon his shoulders, "Cheer you, my gallant friend," he cried, "truthfully you have boldly won the fairest maiden in Christendom."

Christabel's father would have liked to cry out and stop the wedding, but he could not. Neither the old knight nor the Bishop interposed, for they were both so angry that they could not speak. While Friar Tuck proceeded with the ceremony, they both left the church. As soon as all was concluded, the young girls again strewed flowers in the path of the now joyous bride, the bells struck up a merry peal, and the villagers and foresters, rushing out of the church, greeted the happy pair with loud shouts of joy. Robin Hood and his men escorted them home, and having drunk to the welfare and happiness of young Allen-a-Dale and his fair lady, they again returned to their greenwood shades.

So Lady Christabel and Allan-a-Dale were married and went to live in Sherwood Forest with Robin Hood and his merry men. The wedding was often talked about, and the people who were there said it was the prettiest and the merriest wedding they had ever seen. To this day, the ruins of the great abbey in which it took place still stand.

The Bishop of Hereford

Robin Hood would frequently disguise himself and pay visits to the neighboring villages, in order to learn if anything was going on in which he might take a part. In one of these excursions, he overheard a conversation between two priests, by which he learned that the Bishop of Hereford was expected to pass that way very shortly, upon a visit to his not so saintly brother, the Archbishop of York. The outlaw lost no time in ascertaining the route by which the Reverend Father would travel, and with a merry heart he hurried back to his followers in Sherwood Forest. At the sound of his well-known bugle, forty yeomen quickly surrounded him, Little John and Will Scarlet among them.

"We will have noble company to dine with us," said Robin Hood. "Kill a good fat buck or two, and prepare a feast." Three or four foresters quickly darted away to execute this commission.

"Who may it be, master," asked Little John, "that loves to be merry under the greenwood tree?"

"Love or not love," cried the captain laughing, "a noble bishop dines with us today, though he brings a dozen companions with him. But it is time to meet the Reverend Father. You and Will Scarlet attend me, and you too, and you, and you," he added, tapping with his bow the heads of three of his tallest followers, who most willingly complied.

The Bishop of Hereford, as many bishops were in those days, was very rich, very greedy, and exceedingly tyrannical. The nobles regarded him as a powerful cleric, but the people looked upon him with fear, as a proud, overbearing priest.

Upon the occasion of his visit to his brother of York, the Bishop of Hereford rode on horseback, dressed in the white robes of his sacred office. A massive gold chain was suspended round his neck, supporting a golden crucifix, and in his right hand he carried his crosier staff of the same precious metal. His milk-white steed was also richly decorated with silken trappings. The Dean of Hereford, attired in a plain black vestment robe, rode humbly by the side of his superior, who, from time to time, deigned to hold conversation with him upon the vanities of this wicked world. Behind them, twenty horsemen, armed at all points with broadswords by their sides and lances in rest, followed slowly upon chargers of the most jet black, and three or four servants leading pack mules closed the rear. Notwithstanding this entire pompous array, it was with many a misgiving that the Bishop ventured to enter upon the dangerous road through Sherwood Forest.

"Reverend Brother," said he to the Dean, "do you think that the man called Robin Hood will dare to assault the Lord's anointed, if by chance he should have heard of our travels?"

"They say, Reverend Father," replied the Dean, "that he holds the sacred brethren of the church but cheaply and pays but little respect to any of our cloth. I would that we had taken a more meandering route and avoided the paths of this wicked man."

"It is too late to return now," said the Bishop, "and have we not twenty armed men to support us in the hour of trial! Comfort yourself, my brother; with this will I drive off the enemies of our blessed Church," as he flourished his crosier staff above his head. They had proceeded but a short way farther, when suddenly, by the roadside, they came upon six shepherds, dancing merrily round a fire, with which they were cooking venison.

"Ha!" cried the Bishop when he smelled the savory odor from the roasting flesh. "Dare you, villains as you are, slay the King's deer and cook it upon the open road?! For the sake of goodness, you will answer for this."

"Mercy! Mercy, good Bishop!" cried one of the shepherds. "Surely it seems not of your sacred office to take away the lives of so many innocent peasants."

"Guards, seize these villains!" cried the high-ranking cleric, indignant at the presumption of the serf. "Away with them to York; they will be strung on the highest gallows in the city." The armed horsemen turned not over-willingly against the offenders, and endeavored to seize them, but with a loud laugh they darted among the trees, where the steeds could not possibly follow. Presently the shepherd who had begged for mercy pulled from under his frock a little bugle horn and blew a short call upon it. The Bishop and his entourage recoiled with fright and had already begun to urge on their horses, when they found themselves surrounded on every side by archers, dressed in green, with bows drawn in their hands.

"Mercy! Mercy!" cried the Bishop in great trepidation at the sight of fifty or more arrows ready to pierce him through. "Have mercy upon an unfortunate traveler!"

"Fear not, good Father." replied Robin Hood, who was the shepherd that had before spoken. "We do but crave your worshipful company to dine with us under the greenwood tree, and then, when you have paid the forest toll, you will depart in safety." And, stepping into the road, the bold outlaw laid one hand upon the embossed bridle of the Bishop's steed and held the stirrup with the other.

"Oh! That we had but taken the outer road," groaned the Dean to his superior. "We should have avoided these limbs of the evil one."

"Nay, nay Reverend Father," cried Robin Hood, laughing at the poor Bishop's remorseful countenance, "call us not by so bad a name. We do but take from the corrupt rich to administer to the necessities of the poor, and if we do now and then slay a fat buck or two, our good King will never know his loss. But dismount, Holy Sir, and you also, my friends, come likewise. Right merry will we be with such a jovial company."

The horsemen quickly did as they were bidden, but the Bishop most reluctantly unseated himself and, with many a deep sigh, obeyed the injunction of the outlaw. Some of the foresters immediately seized the horses and tied their bridles to the lower branches of the trees, but the pack mules were hurried away through the woods as quickly as the narrow footpaths would allow.

At Robin Hood's command, two young fellows took the unwilling Bishop between them upon their shoulders and, followed by the whole company, bore him to their favorite lawn. A solitary beech tree, whose arms, covered with thick foliage, extended far around, stood in the center, affording a delightful shade from the bright summer sun. Robin Hood seated himself upon one of the twisted roots that grew above the surface of the turf and commanded that his visitor should be brought before him. Little John, taking off his cap as he approached, gently led him to the outlaw, while, to show his spite against him, one of the young foresters had the audacity to tie the cleric's arms behind his back.

A Priestly Quarrel

The entire company, now seated in the company of Robin Hood and his merry men, listened as Robin Hood began to speak. "You are accused of deep crimes," exclaimed Robin. "It is said that you do deal the poor man with a hard hand and show but little mercy to the unfortunate. How do you answer?"

"By what right, mean serf," replied the Bishop, the blood rushing to his temples, "do you question an anointed servant of the Church?"

"Pax vobiscum—peace be with you," cried Friar Tuck, coming forward, and folding his arms in an attitude of defiance. "Why not, good Father? Answer boldly and tell me truthfully that you have never robbed the fatherless and the widow."

"What scolding priest are you?" exclaimed the Bishop. "For your insolence you will be expelled from the Church. Your gown will be stripped from you, and you will be branded as an impostor."

"Save yourself the trouble," replied the Friar, laughing. "The Reverend Abbot of Fountains' Dale has forestalled you in your kind intentions."

"Hold," cried Robin Hood, rising from his seat. "We'll have no more of these priestly quarrels. Reverend Father, accompany us to our meeting tree, and we'll drink to your speedy amendment." Then cutting his bonds with a dagger, he took the arm of his unwilling guest and led him to the spot where they usually partook of their feasts.

Upon the grass was spread a large cloth, covered with provisions of food. Smoking haunches of venison perfumed the air, and huge meat pies baked in pewter vessels, roasted wild swans, peacocks, and a host of minor dishes, filled up any vacancies upon the cloth. At Robin Hood's request, the Bishop said grace, and fifty or more foresters quickly seated themselves to partake of this gallant feast. The cleric, for one in his situation, ate most heartily. His merry host no sooner saw that his platter was empty than he again filled it from the most savory dishes. Wine flowed in abundance, and when, in obedience to Robin Hood, every man filled his goblet to the brim and quaffed its contents to the health of the Bishop of Hereford, the good Father for some moments quite forgot his misfortunes and, striking his palm into the sinewy hand of Robin Hood, swore that he was a jovial fellow.

Many a ballad was then trolled forth by the foresters, and in the excitement of the scene even the Bishop ventured upon a stanza; but, at the moment he had concluded the first verse, his eye caught sight of one of his mules, from whose

back an outlaw was busily removing the trunk that contained his treasure.

"Bring me the calculation, good host," said he meekly, stopping short in his song. "I would happily discharge it and proceed upon my journey."

"Lend me your purse, good Bishop," cried Little John, "and I will save you the trouble."

"Take it," replied the cleric, throwing a very light bag of money to the forester, "and give the surplus to the poor."

"Little John opened the mouth of the purse and emptied out ten golden nobles upon the grass. "And do you think," he exclaimed, laughing heartily at the owner's deplorable countenance, "that a bishop pays no more toll than this? Verily, Reverend Father, the poorest farmer in Nottinghamshire readily grants us so poor a trifle."

"Ho there!" he cried to the man who was disburdening the mules, "bring that trunk here." It was quickly brought and with the help of a broadsword soon opened. Little John first pulled out a handsome cloak, which he spread upon the grass. A gown of the purest white lawn, an ermined robe, and a golden meter were each brought forth in succession and greatly admired by the delighted foresters. But presently a sound metal was heard, and the bold robber drew forth a beautiful ivory casket. The point of a dagger was in a moment applied to the fastening, and treasures invaluable were revealed. The Bishop, who had sat shivering with anxiety during the search, now suddenly sprang to his feet with eager quickness and would have seized his precious wealth had not Robin Hood caught him by the arm.

"Calm yourself, good Father," said the outlaw, "do but fancy that you are distributing this gold in alms to the poor, and you will never be sorry for your charity." The Bishop did not reply but gazed steadfastly on the glittering coins, the sparkling jewels, and the prayer beads that Little John was exhibiting to his companions.

A Merry Dance

"Rouse you, my merry men," cried the chief. "See you not how sad you have made our reverend guest!" A young man quickly brought a simple harp, upon which he struck a lively air, and the gallant outlaw, taking the Bishop by the arm, led him forth, followed by the foresters in pairs. The dance commenced, and the poor cleric, unwilling to provoke his tormentors, joined in the nimble step, which was prolonged till his weary feet could no longer sustain their burden. The Reverend Father fell fairly to the earth from sheer exhaustion.

At Robin Hood's bidding, the two young men again took the Bishop upon their shoulders and bore him to the spot where his steed and those of his entourage were fastened. They placed him upon his saddle backwards, with his face toward the animal's tail instead of the bridle, and they pricked the creature with their daggers, which started it off at full gallop, the terrified rider clinging both with hands and knees to its back. The Dean, the armed horsemen, and the servants were allowed to follow their superior in peace, but the pack mules and their burdens were detained as payment for the feast that had been given to their owners.

IV

A FOURTH ASSEMBLY UPON THE GRASS
OF A MAGNIFICENT PARK

It was, I remember, upon a Saturday afternoon that I was again asked to tell a tale of Robin Hood. On this, the last day of our week of vacation, how great were the pleasures of our holiday! Frequently we had permission granted us to stroll among the fields in the neighborhood in the springtime. And, in the autumn season, we were allowed to pluck the delicious blackberries that, in some places, and we knew them well, abounded among the thorny hedges.

The Wood

At about the distance of a quarter of a mile from our old schoolhouse there was an extensive park. Many hundred acres of land were covered with fine trees—oaks, elms, and firs, variously intermixed—while here and there were open lawns, clothed only with grass and the beautiful wild flowers, that sprang up, uncultivated, in their native soil. An ancient mansion stood in the midst, upon the summit of a hill, whence, looking over the woods; the face of the country for miles around could be traced as upon a map.

The house was deserted; the owner resided in a foreign land, and his noble English park was neglected. It had once been fenced round, but in many places the wooden planks were broken, and a gap made, through which every passenger might enter. We often did, and we chased each other among the crowded thickets. And now, glad of the opportunity of escaping from our confined playground, we went to this delightful park, where, seated upon the grass, with my companions lying around me, I told them the tale of Robin Hood in Finsbury Field.

Robin Hood in Finsbury Field

In the time of Henry the Second and for many years afterwards, until the use of gunpowder was known, the science of archery was greatly encouraged in England among all ranks and classes; and even the good citizens of London constantly exercised their bows in "Finsbury Field." The feast of St. Bartholomew was particularly celebrated by games of this kind. A finely wrought bow or a golden arrow was given as a prize to the best marksman, and the presence of the King and his court contributed not a little to add interest to the long looked-for contests.

One year, towards the close of King Henry's reign, proclamation was as usual made, that the "royal games of archery" would be held in Finsbury Field upon St. Bartholomew's Day. Queen Eleanor of Aquitaine was passionately fond of the sport and rarely missed an opportunity of witnessing the superior skill displayed by the royal archers. She had heard much of Robin Hood but had never seen that gallant outlaw. As the fame of his encounter with the

Bishop of Hereford had spread far and wide, she felt a secret desire to behold so daring and so celebrated a man.

Summoning a young page who waited her commands, the Queen gave him a beautiful golden ring and bade him hasten with all speed to Sherwood Forest and deliver it to the forester with her request that he would come to London and take a part in the approaching games. The youth lost no time in executing his mistress' command and in two days arrived at Nottingham, where, from a good yeoman, he learned the dwelling place of Robin Hood.

On the next morning he appeared before the bold outlaw. Falling gracefully upon one knee, he tipped his cap and presented the ring to him saying, "My royal and most gracious mistress, Eleanor, Queen of England, greets you well. She bids you hasten with all speed to fair London court, that you may be her champion in the sports upon the Feast of St. Bartholomew; in token whereof please accept this ring."

The outlaw took the royal present and placed it upon his finger. "Rise, handsome page," he said, "return upon the fleetest steed that you can find. Deliver this arrow to Queen Eleanor and say that Robin Hood will claim it before three suns have set." The young page rose, placed the arrow in his belt, and with much courtesy bade the outlaw adieu. Then hastening to the inn at Nottingham, he chose the swiftest horse in the stables and flew back again to his royal mistress.

Early in the morning of St. Bartholomew's Day, Finsbury Field presented a merry and most enlivening scene. The large open space, which then existed where streets and squares are now crowded together, was covered with the good citizens of London and their wives and daughters, bedecked in their newest holiday costume. Lanes three hundred yards in length, were marked out in the center of the field, encircled with rails around, to prevent the entrance of the spectators. At one end a scaffold was erected for the accommodation of the King and Queen and their attendants. It was hung with green silk, emblazoned with the royal arms in gold and covered over with a beautiful bright blue cloth, spangled with silver stars. Near it were tents pitched for the use of the contending bowmen, and immediately opposite, at the far end of the lists, a broad target was placed, with a large wooden screen behind it to stop the flight of any stray arrows that did not hit the mark. All were in busy expectation, for the royal party had not yet arrived, and many were the wagers laid upon the favorite archers of Finsbury.

At length a blast of trumpets was heard, and two heralds, dressed in glittering coats of golden silk, with emblazoned banners hanging from their spirit-stirring instruments, entered the ground. The King was mounted on a barbed charger, and the Queen was upon a milk-white riding horse, both magnificently decorated. They appeared amid the waving of caps and the deafening acclamations of the assembled citizens. Next followed, upon steeds of the purest white, a multitude of fair ladies in attendance upon their royal mistress and a band of knights and gentlemen, well mounted and richly dressed, closed the procession.

As soon as the royal party had alighted and had taken their seats upon the gallery, proclamation was made by sound of trumpet that a vat of the best Rhenish wine and a hundred of the fattest hares that ran in "Dallom Chase" would be given to the truest marksman. The archers were then ordered to advance to their posts, and a line was drawn, upon which they were to step when they discharged their arrows. Six bowmen appeared, wearing the King's livery; and marching to the gallery, they tipped their caps to their royal master and took their appointed stations.

"Is there no one," asked King Henry aloud, "is there no bold forester to oppose my gallant archers?"

"A pledge, my Lord, a pledge," cried Queen Eleanor. "Promise me that whoever draws bow on my side will depart uninjured and free for forty days."

"I grant your request, fair Eleanor," replied the King, "but who are these gallant bowmen that require your intercession?"

"Bid the heralds sound again," said Eleanor, "and you will see them." The trumpets again played, and the challenge from the King's archers was repeated.

The Queen's Champion

The Queen waved a light green scarf, and six tall yeomen entered the lanes; advancing to the gallery, they bowed lowly to their royal patroness. One of them, evidently the commander of the little band, was clothed in a rich scarlet doublet and tank hose of the same bright color; a sash of light blue silk, interwoven with threads of gold, crossed his shoulder, supporting his quiver and small golden bugle; and in his hand he carried a most beautifully wrought bow. His companions were dressed in the favorite Lincoln green, and like their commander, each wore a black bonnet with a white streaming feather.

"Welcome, good Locksley," said the Queen, addressing the yeoman in scarlet. "You must draw your best bow for Queen Eleanor." Then turning to the noblemen around her, "Who will support our brave party?" she asked. "My good Lord Bishop of Hereford, will you not in gallantry be on our side?"

"You have six of the best archers of Finsbury to contend against, gracious madam," replied the cleric, "and your men are all strangers. We know not if they can draw a bowstring."

"Will your Grace wager against us?" asked Locksley of the Bishop.

"Ay! By my miter, willingly," returned the Bishop rather warmly. "I'll wager a purse of gold against you and your whole band;" and he drew forth about fifty golden nobles. Locksley replied by throwing upon the turf before the gallery a little bag containing at least an equal quantity of the precious metal, and both stakes were given to the King as umpire of the sport.

The royal archers now took their station upon the line, and one after another let fly an arrow at the broad target. "Why give us such a mark as that?" cried one of them, named Clifton, as his arrow pierced the center. "We'll shoot at the sun and moon."

"Boldly said, my fine fellow," replied Locksley as he drew his bowstring. "You and I will have a bout together presently," and carelessly discharging his arrow, it quivered within a hair's breadth of his opponent's. The spectators, pleased at such fine archery, shouted at the sight, but the King and the Bishop of Hereford could ill conceal their surprise and disappointment. Locksley's men followed, and each one's arrow alighted within a few inches of the center of the target, but so had those of the royal archers.

"The game is equal," said the King, when he had mounted his horse and galloped across the field. "You must shoot again, my brave men. Finsbury has never before seen such archery as this."

"If my gallant friend here," cried Locksley, "who aims at nothing less than bringing down the glorious sun, will but agree to the trial, he and I might decide this contest between ourselves. That is," he continued, "with Your Majesty's royal permission."

"What do you say, Clifton? Are you content to stake your reputation against this braggart's?" asked King Henry.

"Right willingly, my Lord," replied the archer. "I'll lay my own trusty bow against his that he hits not the mark that I do."

"A fair wager," cried Locksley, "which I readily accept."

At the instigation of the champions the broad target was removed, and in its place, a slight willow wand, not above an inch and a half in circumference, was planted firmly in the earth. The spectators gazed with increased wonder. "They surely will not aim at such a mark as that," said they one to another. But the royal bowman stepped to the line and, after carefully adjusting his arrow, let it fly. It peeled off the bark of the wand as it passed by and alighted in the earth a few yards farther on. A loud hooray filled the air, and "Clifton! Clifton!" was shouted from one end of the lists to the other.

The merry yeoman Locksley did not wait till these cries had subsided. "I will notch his shaft," he said aloud as he advanced composedly to his post; and fitting his arrow, he drew the bowstring to his ear and, after one moment's deliberation, discharged the weapon with his utmost force. The shaft flew true and, to the amazement of the beholders, split that of his opponent.

At first a deep silence prevailed. Many could not see where the arrow had struck, and some were dumb with astonishment; but when one of the attendants pulled it forth, a shout of applause was raised, so loud, so long, and so vehement, that those of the good citizens of London who had remained at home rushed forth from the gates in hundreds to inquire the cause of so violent

an outbreak.

The King's vexation at this defeat of his party quickly changed into admiration of Locksley's superior skill. He rode up to his side. "Will you be one of my archers?" he asked. "A hundred pounds a year, the free use of my pantry, and a new suit of livery every three months will be your reward."

"It grieves me, my Lord," replied the yeoman, "that I cannot comply with your request, but grant me one request, and I and my gallant men will support you to our deaths."

"Name it, good Locksley. It is already granted," said the King.

"Pardon, most gracious lord, pardon for the outlawed Robin Hood and his brave followers."

"And are you Robin Hood," asked Henry, his countenance flushed with anger, "whose defiance of the law has filled the whole North Country with alarm? It is certain, you are the boldest villain that ever shot a bow. Ho! Guards there, take charge of this over-valiant knave."

The Outlaw's Pardon

"Remember your promise," cried a gentle voice from the gallery. "Remember you have pledged your honor."

King Henry turned as he recognized the sweet tones of his lovely consort, and a smile played upon his lips as he replied, "It was but in jest, fair Eleanor, it was but in jest. We will willingly grant pardon to you and your followers," he continued to the outlaw, "if you will forsake your unlawful pursuits and lead the sober lives of honest yeomen."

"We cannot quit the greenwoods of Sherwood," said Robin Hood, "but if your majesty will grant us leave to range the forest and now and then exercise our archery upon one of the thousands of fat deer that bound so gaily over the lawns, we will promise that no traveler will again complain of the outlaws of Nottinghamshire."

The King bit his lips in silence, but at that moment the defeated archer advanced and tendered his bow to the victor.

"You are a good marksman, Clifton," said the King. "If you had made a little more allowance for the distance, your arrow would not have passed the wand. Keep your bow, man, though I tell it to you, there's but one better archer in merry England."

"If I had known that you were Robin Hood," cried the Bishop of Hereford, as the King delivered the well-filled purses to the outlaw, "I would not have wagered against you. You have already had more gold of mine than I ever intended."

"Surely you do not forget the jovial dinner we gave you under our meeting tree," replied Robin Hood. "Yet if you do begrudge the payment, I will return it even now."

"Nay, nay, master," cried Little John, who had accompanied his captain, "that would be unwise, since you have promised not to relieve travelers of their superfluous wealth. It is folly not to keep all the gold you come honestly by."

Robin Hood with a smile threw the purses to his more considerate follower, bowed low to the King and still lower to his fair patroness, and accompanied by his five merry yeomen, departed from the field.

Sherwood Forest soon rang again with the sound of his bugle horn, but the promise given on Finsbury Field was kept during King Henry the Second's lifetime, and no traveler had reason to complain of the bold outlaws. This did not last, however, for the throne changed, and with it the rule of law.

The Knight of Wierysdale

We must suppose that several years had elapsed since Robin Hood's victory in Finsbury Field, when the following tale commences. Richard the Lionheart had succeeded to his father Henry the Second's throne, and with many of his nobles had joined the memorable Crusades. During his absence, the internal state of England had become far worse than it was at the time of his accession. His brother Prince John ruled in his absence but not honestly. Baron rose up against baron, and princes made war upon each other, till discord, tumult, and fierce plunder reigned throughout the land. It was not, therefore, to be wondered at, when the laws were for a time suspended, and force of arms alone decided the contest, that the bold foresters had again resorted to their superior strength.

It was a bright morning in early summer, when a solitary horseman was proceeding upon his journey through one of the narrow roads that crossed Barnesdale forest.

All dreary was his semblance,
And little was his pride;
His one foot in the stirrup stood,
The other waved beside;

His hood was hanging o'er his eyes,
He rode in simple array;
A sorrier man than he was one
Rode never on summer's day.

A deep sigh escaped from the melancholy horseman, and big tears coursed down his cheeks at every step of his poor lean beast. When three men suddenly emerged from the wood, and stood before his path, he seemed scarcely conscious of their presence.

"God save you, Sir Knight," cried one of them, a tall forester nearly seven feet high, moved with compassion at his forlorn appearance. "Welcome to our merry greenwood. You must be our guest today."

"Leave me, good sirs, I pray you," said the Knight mournfully, "my sorrows are already too heavy for me to bear. Add not to my distress."

"No, do not be so downcast," returned the former speaker. "You are in good hands, and you may trust us. Our master waits dinner for a guest, and you are the first man who has passed through Barnesdale this day." Then taking the Knight's rein in his hand, the forester led the jaded steed through the intricate paths of the wood, until he arrived at an open lawn, where a band of yeomen were reclining under the shade of a huge elm.

"Welcome, Sir Knight," said one of them rising and tipping his cap at the appearance of a stranger. "Welcome to merry Barnesdale."

"Who are you," inquired the horseman, "that causes travelers to be constrained from their way? I am but a poor knight, without so much as a piece of gold, wherewith to buy me food."

"More welcome still," exclaimed the forester, assisting him from his horse. "We will have the blessings of charity upon our deeds. You have heard of Robin Hood to be sure. I am that outlaw, and these are my gallant followers."

"Unless report belie you," replied the Knight, "you are a friend to the unfortunate. Dismiss me at once, and let me speed on."

Robin's Generosity toward the Knight

"Dine with us first," said the forester, "and freely will you depart." A cloth was spread beneath the shady branches and covered with a profusion of the most delicious provisions. Rhenish wine and ale plentifully abounded and with cheerful hearts, about twenty yeomen seated themselves around. "Eat gladly, Sir Knight," said Robin Hood. "Here's to your health and a more merry countenance," and as he spoke he consumed the contents of a goblet.

"Thanks, thanks, my noble host," replied the stranger. "It grieves me that I will never be able to return your goodness."

"Truly, good sir, you look but grievous," answered the outlaw. "Tell me, is there anything in which my services can avail you? What is the cause of your deep sorrow?"

"I have lost land and gold," returned the Knight, "and I fear that my good name must follow them." His tears burst out afresh. "They call me," he continued, "Sir Richard of the Lee. I am sprung of noble blood, and for these last three hundred years have my ancestors worn spurs. Twelve short months ago I had a noble house and fine estate with four hundred pounds a year, but now, except for my lovely wife and my children, I have nothing in the world."

"How have you lost your riches?" inquired Robin Hood anxiously.

"It is a short story," replied the Knight. "I fought in a fair field with a knight of Lancashire and slew him. To save my liberty, I mortgaged the broad lands of Wierysdale to St. Mary's Abbey, and if I pay not the amount tomorrow, my castle will be forfeited."

"What is the sum you owe, and what will you do if you lose your land?" asked the outlaw.

"Four hundred golden pounds must I pay if I would keep fair Wierysdale," he replied. "I go to beg grace for another year. If the Reverend Abbot will not grant it, I must flee away across the broad seas to a country where they know me not."

"Where are your friends?" asked Little John. "Will they not be security for you?"

"Alas," replied Sir Richard, "when I had money and house and lands, I lacked not the means; but now my oldest companions turn from me as a herd of deer would from a poor wounded hare. My only trust is in God."

"Who will be surety for you?" asked the outlaw. "Truthfully, good sir, you must find wealthy friends."

"I have none other," replied the Knight mournfully, "except God, who in all my trials has never failed me."

"You have indeed a good friend," said Robin Hood, "and if you will promise that in twelve months from this day it will be restored to me, I will lend you what you want." The Knight fell upon his knees, gave the required promise, and drawing forth a silver cross, kissed it.

In the meanwhile Little John had gone to the outlaws' treasury and now returned with a heavy bag. He quickly counted out four hundred pieces of gold and offered them to the Knight with a beautiful doublet of scarlet cloth. These he readily accepted. At Robin Hood's bidding, a gallant grey steed with regal trappings was next brought forth, and after having received a pair of golden spurs from the hands of the noble outlaw, the Knight vaulted into the saddle.

"It would be a shame," said Robin Hood, "that so well equipped a knight should ride without esquire. I will lend you my brave man, Little John, until you get a yeoman for your service." The forester willingly agreed, and mounting a stout riding horse, he was soon ready to accompany his new master. With tears of joy instead of sorrow, the Knight bid farewell to his kind and generous host, struck his spurs into his new charger, and followed by Little John, galloped swiftly over the plain.

The Abbot of St. Mary's Abbey

On the morning after this adventure, the Reverend Superior of St. Mary's Abbey, in the old city of York, was seated in his hall, attended by several of the monks.

"Upon this day twelve months ago," said he to his attentive listeners, "there came a knight who borrowed four hundred pounds, upon the security of his lands and castle. The hour is near at hand. Unless he appears and pays the money before that glass has run out, the fair lands of Wierysdale will belong to this sanctuary."

"It is early yet, Reverend Father," replied his deputy. "The poor man may be in a far country, and it would be unwise to use him harshly. I think your conscience, my Lord Abbot, would but ill bear so rude a treatment to an unfortunate knight."

"You are ever in my beard," exclaimed the Superior angrily. "I declare that, unless the Knight of Wierysdale appears before the sun has set, he will be disinherited."

"He is either dead, or he cannot pay," said a fat monk, who was high cook, "and St. Mary's Abbey will be enriched with a goodly sum. Shall I not seek the Lord Justice, Reverend Father, and bid him attend to prepare deeds for the transfer of the land?"

"Yes, brother," replied the Abbot. "It is but lost time to wait for our debtor, therefore use dispatch, good brother, use dispatch." The cook left the room as quickly as his fat limbs would carry him, and in less than an hour returned with the Lord Chief Justice.

In the mean time Sir Richard of the Lee and his esquire had arrived in York and taken up their abode at an inn. After they had rested for a while from the fatigue of their journey, they dressed themselves in their sorriest attire and set out to the Abbey. Upon knocking at the great gates, they were immediately admitted and conducted into a lofty and spacious room, whose high pointed roof ornamented with grotesque images, narrow Gothic windows, and beautifully tessellated pavement combined to strike the beholder with admiration and increase his reverence for the inmates of such a noble dwelling.

The Knight and his attendant tipped their caps and bowed low as they entered the hall, and they advanced to the upper end, where, upon a carved oak throne, sat the Abbot of St. Mary's Abbey, with the Lord Chief Justice of

York by his side.

"God save you, Reverend Father," said the Knight, as he kneeled before him. "I have attended you this day as you did bid me."

"Have you brought any money, Sir Knight?" asked the priest in a harsh tone.

"Not one penny," replied the suppliant. "I am come to beg that you will extend the time of payment for one more year."

"That is unfortunate," rejoined the Abbot, with difficulty repressing his delight at the intelligence. "The day is nearly gone, and unless you can pay down four hundred pounds before the setting of the sun, your lands must pass to the accruement of St. Mary's Abbey. Sir Justice," he continued, looking distrustfully, "here's to you," and in the height of his satisfaction he emptied a goblet of wine at a single draught.

"Good Sir Justice," said the Knight imploringly, "will you not assist me in my distress. Day by day will I serve you until I have repaid your goodness."

"No, Sir," returned the Justice, "I cannot do it if I had the will. Give him two hundred pounds more, Reverend Father, and the good Knight will sign you a release of the lands that he can no longer claim."

"Never!" replied the Knight fiercely, as he started to his feet. "Merciless tyrants as you are, you get not my lands. Never will monk or friar be heir to Wierysdale."

"What?" cried the priest, rising from his seat. "Do you dare oppose the Abbot of St. Mary's? Out with you false Knight, your castle is no longer yours."

"You lie," returned the Knight stamping his heel upon the pavement until it rung again. "Never was I false. I've stood in tournaments against noble earls and greater men than you, and I have often proven myself a true and good Knight. Take back your gold," he continued, as he poured out the contents of his purse at the Abbot's feet, "and think not that you can so easily get the fair lands of Wierysdale. Had you shown courtesy to a suppliant knight, you should have had recompense." Then snatching away the papers which the Justice had before him, Sir Richard darted a look of defiance at the Abbot, and with a firm step departed from the hall, leaving an astonished and baffled Reverend Father.

Sir Richard returned to his inn, gave away his old garments to the first beggar that passed by, and after dismissing his gallant esquire with the warmest thanks for his assistance, again started off with an attendant whom Little John had procured for him. He rode on, singing merrily, until he drew rein at his own gate in Wierysdale. His lady, with tears in her eyes, had been watching his approach, but when she saw the joyful countenance and proud bearing of her husband, she ran forth to clasp him in her arms and to learn the cause of such unexpected joy, joined by their children, all with happy faces. The story was briefly told, and from that day to the end of their lives the good Knight and his lady did not fail to remember in their prayers the name of Robin Hood.

The Revenge of the Bishop of Hereford

The Bishop of Hereford was very angry with Robin Hood for the tricks he had played on him, especially in kidnapping him, taking his gold, and sending him away in ridicule backwards on horseback. He was so angry that he would have been very pleased if anyone had caught Robin. But no one did. The wicked people were nearly all afraid of Robin and his brave men. The people who were kind and good loved him.

One day the Bishop had to take a great deal of money to a monastery, and he had to pass through Sherwood Forest. He felt sure he would meet Robin Hood, so he gathered together all his servants and as many soldiers as he could. He hoped either to kill Robin or to take him prisoner and to bring him to Nottingham to have him hanged there.

He hoped most to take him prisoner, because he knew his friend, the Sheriff of Nottingham, was Robin's greatest enemy and had promised to give a large sum of money to anyone who would take Robin prisoner.

It was a bright, sunshiny day in the middle of June when the Bishop set out. It was cool and shady under the great leafy trees of the forest. Wild roses and blue morning glory trailed across the path. The banks and ditches were bright with yellow pennywort and tansy. Sweetbrier and honeysuckle scented the air. Birds sang and twittered in the branches, and all the world was full of beauty.

Into the still and peaceful forest rode the Bishop and his men. Soon the woody paths were filled with the noise of neighing and trampling horses. The clang of swords and the clatter and jingle of steel harness and armor frightened the deer in their lairs and the birds in their nests.

But it was a splendid sight to see all these bold soldiers in shining armor riding along. The Bishop rode in the middle of them, wearing a magnificent robe, trimmed with lace, over his armor.

Robin loved to roam in the forest, and he would often leave his men and wander off by himself. This morning everything was so bright and beautiful that he went on and on, hearing nothing but the songs of birds, seeing nothing but the trees and flowers.

Suddenly he saw the Bishop and his men riding down a wide forest path. They, too, saw him quite plainly, for he was standing right in the middle of the path, looking up into a tree, listening to a black bird singing. He knew that one man singly, however brave he might be, could not fight against all these soldiers. Nor could he call his men by blowing his horn, as he generally did when he was in danger, for they were so far away. It was a dreadful moment.

With wild shouts of triumph the Bishop and his men were riding down upon him. There was only one thing to do. And Robin did it. He ran away.

Fast and faster he ran, closely followed by the Bishop's men. In and out among the trees he went, twisting and turning. After him came the soldiers, shouting wildly. He led them into the thickest part of the wood. Closer and closer grew the trees, narrower and narrower the pathways. Horses stumbled over roots or trailing branches of ivy, sending their riders sprawling on the ground. There they lay, unable to rise, because of the weight of their heavy armor. The overhanging branches of the trees caught others and knocked them off their horses, which galloped away riderless and terrified far into the forest.

It was a mad and breathless chase. Robin knew every path and secret way in all the woods. The trees seemed to bend down to hide him as he passed and spread out their gnarled roots to trip up the horses of the Bishop's men.

Robin's suit, too, of Lincoln green, was almost the color of the leaves in summer, and that helped him. The men found it more and more difficult to follow, and at last they lost him altogether.

The Old Woman's Disguise

Robin could hear the shouts of the Bishop's men growing fainter and fainter in the distance, but still he ran on. He knew the danger was not yet over. In the very thickest part of the wood he came to an old woman's cottage. He often sent presents to this poor old woman, so he was sure she would help him.

Knocking loudly on the door, he called, "Open, open quickly and let me in."

The old woman hobbled to the door and opened it as fast as she could. "Who are you?" she said as she looked upon this guest in distress. Robin told her quickly that the Bishop and all his men were on his trail and would have his head unless she helped him.

"Come in," said the old woman, plucking him by the sleeve. "Come in quickly."

Robin stepped into the house. The old woman shut and bolted the door after him.

"If you are really Robin Hood,' said she, looking at him hard, "I'll do anything I can to hide you from the Bishop and his men."

"I am truly Robin Hood, my good woman. If you help me, neither my men nor I will ever forget it."

"I believe you, sir, I believe you. You have an honest face," answered the old woman. "And I'm not likely to forget all the kindness I have had from you and your merry men. Why, no later than last Saturday night you sent me a pair of shoes and some fine woolen stockings. See," she added, putting out one foot, "I'm wearing the shoes at this very minute. But haste you, lad, hurry," she went on more quickly. Where will you hide?

"Give me a gray dress and a big white cap like those you wear. Dressed in them I can go safely through the wood till I meet my men. If I do chance to come across the Bishop and his soldiers I will hobble along like any old woman, and they will never stop to look at me. Then you put on my suit of Lincoln green. If the Bishop follows me here, as I think he will, he will mistake you for me. Let him take you prisoner, and do not be afraid, for my good fellows and I will soon be back to rescue you from him."

"Bless your life, sir, what a head you have," said the old woman laughing. Then she got the clothes for Robin.

Disguised as the old woman, Robin left her home and made his way to his company. Once he met several of the Bishop's men, but he bent his back and hobbled slowly along, muttering and mumbling to himself till they were out of sight.

It took him a long time to get where his own men were. For one thing he found it was very difficult to walk in a dress. On the other hand, he was afraid to go too fast in case he should be seen by any of the Bishop's people.

At last he got to the place where he had left his men. There stood Little John looking out for him. Robin waved his stick and shouted, but he was so well disguised that his great friend did not know him.

"Look at that strange creature," said Little John to Will Scarlet who stood beside him. "What is it? Who is it?" said Will.

Coming closer, the creature said, "It is I, Robin Hood!"

Little John, taken back, said, "Master, master, what has happened that you have come back in this guise? You are wearing a…a dress!"

Robin soon told all his tale. Then he said, "We must gather our men and fight the Bishop to save this good old woman." Robin quickly changed his clothes and dressed in Lincoln green, then led his men in search of the Bishop.

The old woman had barely enough time to get into Robin's clothes before the Bishop arrived. He was sure Robin would take refuge in her cottage. He called with furious mood, "Come let me soon see, and bring unto me that traitor Robin Hood!"

The old woman never said a word. She let them shout and bang at her door as much as they liked. With Robin's hat pulled well down over her face, she stood in a dark corner and waited. After a great deal of noise they burst the door open and rushed in. They shouted with triumph when they saw the figure in green standing in the corner.

The old woman had armed herself with a good stout stick. Though she hobbled when she walked, her late husband had taught her how to give a stiff blow against any who threatened her. With this stick she laid about her, making a great show of fighting. She did indeed give one or two of the Bishops' men hearty smacks on the head. The noise was tremendous. Outside she could hear the Bishop shouting, "Gently, my men, gently. Take him alive, take him alive."

After a little time, she pretended to give in and allowed several of the men to tie her hands behind her back. They led her out to the Bishop. So glad was he to see Robin Hood, as he thought, captured and bound, that he rocked in his saddle for very joy.

"Aha, my man," he cried, we have you at last. Say farewell to your greenwood. You will never see it again."

The woman held her head down, though her hat was pulled well over here face, for fear the Bishop would find out that she was not Robin Hood at all.

But the Bishop was so old and blind that he could not tell that it was not Robin. Besides, he was so sure that he had got him that he hardly even looked at the old woman's face. He thought Robin was hanging his head in shame.

"Ho there," he cried, "Honor to the prince of thieves; bring the finest horse in the company for the King of Sherwood Forest."

So a milk-white horse, the finest in all the company, was brought forward. Two men helped the old woman on to it. They tied her on firmly in case she should try to jump off and run away. They wondered how such a manly rebel as Robin could weigh so little, but their excitement over capturing Robin overruled their common sense, and they discovered not her guise.

"He is ugly enough anyhow," said one man, looking at the old woman.

"As ugly as sin," said another.

"Ah, my children," said the Bishop, who heard them, "you see what sin does. This man leads a wicked life, and it has left its mark on his face."

When the old woman heard that, she shook with anger, for it was so untrue. But the Bishop thought that Robin was trembling in fear. "Ah, you may well tremble, my man," he said. "The punishment of all your wicked deeds is near." Yet the woman never answered a word.

"Sound the trumpet," said the Bishop, turning to the captain of his soldiers. "Call in all our scattered men, for I would be at St. Mary's Abbey by noon."

So the trumpet was sounded, and all the Bishop's servants and soldiers gathered together again. Once more they set off, the old woman on her beautiful white horse riding beside the Bishop on his dapple-gray pony.

As they rode along, the Bishop laughed and sang for joy. He was so glad that he had taken Robin Hood prisoner. His laughter did not last long, however. For as they were riding, he chanced to see a hundred brave bowmen stout and strong headed his way.

"Who are these," said the Bishop, "and what man is that who leads them?"

Then, for the first time, the old woman spoke. "Faith," said she, "I think it is a man called Robin Hood."

The Bishop made his horse stop, and laying a hand on the old woman's reins turned to her with a pale face. "Who are you, then?" he asked.

"Only an old woman, my Lord Bishop. Only an old woman and not Robin Hood at all," she replied.

"Then woe is me," the Bishop said, and he turned to go, but not before Robin and his men were upon him.

"No, my Lord Bishop," said Robin, taking his hat off and bowing politely, "no, my Lord, you cannot go yet. You owe us something for all the trouble you have given us."

Then he went to the old woman, unbound her hands, and lifted her gently to the ground. "I thank you, dame," he said, "for your kindness to me this day. Robin Hood will never forget it. Now you must have more comfortable clothes. If you follow Much the miller' son, he will take you to Lady Christabel. She is waiting for you to enhance your wardrobe, in appreciation for your kindness.

"Thank you kindly," said the old woman, as she went away giggling, "but I think I'll take to wearing Lincoln green myself, for green is my favorite color."

The Bishop's Joy Turned to Sorrow

The Bishop's men did not attempt to fight. They saw it was useless. Robin had gathered so many of his brave men that they could easily have killed all the Bishop's men if they had tried. So they laid down their swords and spears and waited quietly to see what would happen next. Robin helped the Bishop get off his horse and gave him a comfortable seat on the root of a tree. Then seating himself opposite he said, "Now, my Lord Bishop, how much money have you with you?"

"The money which I have with me is not mine," replied the Bishop.

"Very true it is not yours," agreed Robin, smiling.

"It belongs to the Monastery of St. Mary," said the Bishop.

"Pardon me, it belongs to the poor people from whom you have stolen it," said Robin sternly, "to whom it is now going to be returned. Little John, bring the Bishop's money bags."

Little John brought the Bishop's money bags and counted our five hundred pounds upon the ground.

"Now let him go," said Robin. He called for the Bishop's horse. He set him on it and led him and his men back to the broad path through the woods.

There he took leave of them. "Go," he said to the Bishop, "thank God for all His mercies to you this day, and in your prayers forget not Robin Hood." Then they departed, but much in despair.

"Master," said Little John, "it is a long time since we have had a service of thanksgiving under the arch."

"You are right," said Robin. "Friar Tuck will lead us in thanksgiving, for we have seen great mercies today."

So in the dim wood, beneath the tall trees that formed an archway overhead, as if they had been in a great cathedral, Robin and his men sang songs of worship and knelt together in prayer. The birds joined in the singing and the trees whispered the amens.

I had just finished this tale, when the chimes from the distant steeple faintly reached our ears. The ringing decorated our imagination as if we ourselves were in the forest cathedral. But we were reminded that the hour at which we were expected back had arrived, and we were at least a quarter of an hour's walk away. We started to our feet, bounded through the wood and over the low palings, and made many a passenger laugh heartily as we chased past him to our home.

V

OUR FIFTH GATHERING
IN THE SHRUBBERY

This evening we resumed our old seats under the sycamore tree in the shrubbery, which by this time had become our own meeting tree, and I continued my tales.

Robin Meets Maid Marian

It was spring in Sherwood. Flowers were budding, and their fragrance filled the air. It was not often that the merry men of Sherwood thought of anything but the keen delights of the chase, the goodly joys of archery, the manly cheer of the quarterstaff play; but it was spring, and at times their minds turned towards other things and other days.

Now it was at this time, while Robin Hood was leading his men in Sherwood and living the life of a bold outlaw, that his mind occasionally wandered to memories of someone whom he had known from his boyhood long ago—Maid Marian. "I wonder whether she ever heard of my outlawry, or if she remembers me. We were but boy and girl, yet never since have I seen a maid that compares to her.

Marian was the daughter of upright parents whose house had stood near Robin's childhood home. Robin and Marian had been close comrades during their childhood. They had played together, hunting for birds' nests, fishing in the brook, climbing trees, or running races over the meadow grass. They even learned together the use of bow and arrow, having contests in the acreage near their homes, with Marian occasionally taking the prize. Years had passed since those days of merriment.

When Robin was forced into outlawry, he managed the lives of many—many who admired him and followed him. Still there were times of seclusion that gave occasion for thought and contemplation—reflection on life's purpose and on family. On days when the forest rang loudly with still quiet, he would lie on the moss and think about his merry childhood and of Maid Marian, his dear friend. He did not know that events had gone very poorly for Marian. Her parents were honest and true in all things, but they were Saxon, so when Norman officials came to collect taxes, they were practically robbed of all they had—all except their only child, their lovely daughter Marian.

With no grain and little food, her mother, trying to care for her family and personally sacrificing for their welfare, became ill and died. The father also worked long and hard hours to provide for his only child, Maid Marian. But the hardship of unjust taxation had taken a toll. He felt his days were not long, and he knew he could not provide what she needed. Being a young lady by now, he thought that Robin Hood's band could better care for her than he. On a particular evening after their meager supper, sitting by the hearth, he told Marian to find Robin Hood. Looking into her searching eyes he said, "Robin is an honorable, gallant, and noble man—a man of good heart, stalwart in holding forth truth and righteousness. He will care for you as I cannot. For a long time we have not known where he was, but at last his name rings through the country; he has become the renowned outlaw of whose daring deeds minstrels sing and of whom men talk as they sit about the evening fire." Marian listened quietly. She knew her father's words rang with wisdom and understanding, though the thought of leaving her father filled her heart with sadness.

After time and thought, Marian resolved to heed her father's counsel and to seek Robin Hood in Sherwood Forest; but she feared leaving her father, now older and alone. Nevertheless, by his urging, she prepared to go. She and her father both knew how unsafe it was for a lady to travel about the country alone;

the danger of robbers or other harm was real. She put on the dress of a page, with a hood that covered her head, took quiver and bow, sword and buckler; thus armed and disguised, she gave a sad farewell to her father and set out to seek Robin.

At last she reached the skirts of the great forest, and as soon as she entered the dark shades of the mighty oaks she looked eagerly for the first sign of a forest dweller who could direct her to the haunts of her old friend.

On this same day, Robin had set out alone on an expedition in search of adventure. He had taken great care to disguise himself, for his fate would be certain if he fell into the hands of the King's foresters, given command by the Sheriff of Nottingham to show no mercy to Robin Hood or his men. He had chosen to wear a cloak and hood of sober brown, but he still wore his sword and carried his bow and quiver. He pulled the hood well over his brows and about his face, so that even one of his own men would have scarcely recognized him. His tattered cloak huddled over his shoulders as he went out.

Thus disguised, he strode briskly through the forest, glancing keenly from side to side as he went, to see whether there were any traces of game. Presently he saw indications that a deer had passed, and he crept cautiously along, one hand grasping his bow, the other just ready to draw an arrow from his quiver. He saw the game at last, a noble animal grazing in an open space. Quick as a flash, Robin raised his bow, the arrow poised for flight. With his usual seemingly careless aim, he shot. At the same instant he was astonished to hear the twang of a second bowstring, the whiz of another arrow. As the deer fell dead, it was impossible to tell for a moment which arrow had caused the killing. Robin ran forward, and saw another lad bounding from the trees directly opposite—the figure of a handsomely dressed stripling coming along the way towards him. This young boy seemed to be entirely alone. And Robin did not recognize him.

"My game!" cried the boy in a high voice.

"Nay, that you must prove!" replied Robin, rather sharply, for he prided himself, and with good reason, upon his shooting, and it displeased him that this stripling should have had a better aim than he. He bent over the dying deer, and to his chagrin, he found that it was indeed the stranger's arrow that was causing the animal's death.

"You are right; 'tis thy game," he began courteously if coldly. "But who are you and what do you want in Sherwood?" demanded Robin Hood.

Marian, disguised as the lad, also did not recognize Robin and thought him to be some savage highwayman who would likely plunder her, so she sprang back and laid her hand on her sword. "This is not one of Robin's men," she thought. "This is some footpad whom I must meet boldly or I am undone." So she said, "Stand aside, fellow, and let me go on my way. I have nothing to do with you."

"Ay, but I may have something to do with you," replied the tattered stranger. "Tell me where and why you go through the forest, or I must turn you back."

"Turn me back?" said the page, "That will you never do. Put me not to the need of drawing sword in my defense, as go back I will not."

Robin thought that the sight of his blade would frighten a mere lad, so he drew his sword out and sprang forward, making a lunge. But, to his surprise, the lunge was deftly turned aside, and the slender page met him as boldly with sword and buckler as ever Robin had met.

Their swords clashed, and though Robin did not exert the whole of his strength and skill against a mere lad, the page was not all unskilled in sword play, for on one occasion Robin's guard was passed, and he received a small wound in the face. The outlaw admired this brave young opponent and tried to make a peaceful end to their fray.

"Hold your hand," said Robin, "and you shall range the forest with bold Robin Hood and his men."

"What! Robin Hood?" cried the page. "Are you indeed Robin Hood? You are he whom I seek."

"Why, who are you?" Robin said.

Pulling her hood back, she said, "Robin, don't you know me?"

"Maid Marian! How did you happen to come to Sherwood dressed as a boy page?"

The two friends now sat down on a mossy bank near at hand and fell into talk, telling each other how their lives had passed since their separation, Robin

explaining his outlawry and Marian sharing her father's counsel, saying, "Have you room for me in the greenwood, Robin?"

"Come, we will seek Lady Christabel, the wife of Allen-a-Dale; she will gladly take you under her care." So they set off together and sought the hidden glade where the band formed their camp. And right welcome did Christabel make Maid Marian. She was safe; and feeling secure, she lay down in peace and slept.

Some time passed, and Marian found her place in the work and daily routine of life in the greenwoods of Sherwood. She helped with domestic duties as well as hunting, and with Mrs. Allen-a-Dale, helped make the forest a home away from home for many. This did not go unnoticed by Robin who found himself drawn to Marian, which was not be surprising because of her great beauty and noble character. They spent time together, often hunting or walking through wooded paths speaking of their merry childhood but also of how much life had changed since then. They had so much to say to each other that the time went all too quickly. Over the course of time betrothal was eminent, and it was right that Robin Hood and Maid Marian should marry.

The Wedding of Maid Marian and Robin Hood

The day was set, the bridegroom ready to take his bride. Marian wore a fine dress that was discovered among several in a bale of goods, which a wealthy merchant left with Robin and the merry men to express his appreciation for the kindnesses they showed him in his travels through the greenwoods. The dress was glittering white, and over it a robe of lovely satin, green and shimmering like beech leaves in early spring. Her dark hair was caught up in a net of pearls, and a soft white veil fell about her face. At sight of her, Robin, standing tall and blissful in his Lincoln greens adorned with a white feather in his lapel, drew in his breath, saying, "I had not known that anyone could look so beautiful."

The day was lovely, a day for joy, and the wedding as beautiful as any forest could adorn in the great cathedral of the arching wildwood. All Robin's men attended, and as they passed Robin, every man, dressed in Lincoln green, bowed. Then each one knelt on one knee, kissing Marian's hand, and vowing to serve and honor her as his queen. And so every man went to his place, and Marian stood gazing at them all as they passed.

The fat and jolly Friar Tuck officiated with his big book, trying to look grave, using a rustic altar which he had built soon after he had joined the band. Little John was the best man, with the wife of Allen-a-Dale as Marian's matron of honor. A hush fell upon everyone while Robin and Marian knelt together exchanging vows of love and honor, and the new couple, held in high esteem by all of the forest, became man and wife. Upon their rising, the assembled company raised a great shout of admiration.

Following the wedding, a celebration began with a feast of good proportion. Right merry was this feast, which was held in the glade under the clear sky with sunlight shining through the opening in the canopy. Little John and Allen-a-Dale had earlier embarked with their bows and killed a brace of fat bucks especially for this joyous feast, held in honor of the marriage of Robin Hood and Maid Marian. The yeoman formed a jovial ring around a vast fire of great oak billets, ate their fill of the sweet venison, and washed it down with flagons of wine and brimming bowls of nut-brown ale. The cooks had done their very best and had made all the most delightful dishes. The tablecloths, which were spread upon the grass, were strewn with wildflowers. Happy talk and laughter rang merrily through the wood.

When the feast was over, Robin filled his drinking horn, and holding it high above his head said, "Here's a health to Maid Marian, Queen of the Green Wood." It was a fine sight to see all his men as they sprang to their feet. They looked so handsome and tall in their coats of Lincoln green. They waved their hats and cheered for Maid Marian, till the forest echoed again.

"Here's to fair Maid Marian and bold Robin Hood," they cried. "Long may they live, and happy may they be together."

Everyone was joyful and merry. Only Little John felt the least bit sad. "Now that Robin has such a lovely wife, he will not need his friend anymore," he said sorrowfully to himself.

But Maid Marian saw that he looked sad, and guessing why, she talked kindly to him, and soon he was as merry as the rest. They sang and danced and

played, and no one seemed to tire.

So this happy day of feasting and merry celebration came to an end. The red sun sank behind the trees. The birds slept, and all the forest was silent; only the bright stars were awake, which watched over Robin and his bride. Sherwood now had a rightful queen who reigned with dignity and grace. She would be a good wife for Robin, faithfully supporting him in his valiant efforts to right the many wrongs of their time.

Reynolde Grenelefe

Not long after the wedding of Robin and Marian, Little John determined to seek an adventure that he might have something to boast of among his companions when he returned to Barnesdale woods. By chance he learned that there was to be a grand archery meeting near Nottingham and that the High Sheriff was to award a prize to the best marksman. Without delay, he rode across the country bypaths, which no one but a daring forester would have chosen, and upon the next morning reached the appointed ground, just as the sports were about to commence.

The best bowmen of the county had entered the lists, and as a silver bugle horn was to be awarded to the victor, each man had resolved to do his best to gain it. Upon the appearance of the new competitor, they looked at each other and, after whispering together, laughed at the presumption of the lowly stranger, who had dared to offer himself as their rival.

One by one the well-known and often victorious archers advanced and shot their arrows so near the center of the target that it was next to impossible to say whose aim had been the truest. Little John shot last and with such success that his arrow knocked out one of the very nearest of his opponents. The Sheriff, surprised at his dexterity, rode forth, examined the target and declared that he could not pronounce a decision. At the suggestion of the forester, to whom the others now paid greater respect, a thick white wand, which a ranger had been using to keep back the spectators, was placed upright in the ground at twenty paces farther distance.

Again the sports began. The Nottingham men supported their reputation, and no less than three arrows stuck in the mark. The outlaw fired last and also hit the wand. These four again shot, when two of the bowmen missed, and the contest remained to be decided between the first marksman of Nottingham and the bold stranger.

The populace had often given vent to their admiration of such gallant archery by loud hoorays, but now a breathless silence prevailed. The Sheriff, anxious for the honor of his county, rode up and down in a perfect fever of excitement and spoke encouraging words to the Nottingham champion. The man coolly took up his position and drew his bow with the greatest care, but the shaft unfortunately flew half an inch above the mark. Little John smiled, advanced, and shot his arrow a third time into the middle of the wand. A feeling of disappointment seemed to spread over the spectators, and the defeated archer could ill conceal his chagrin.

"Tell me, my good friend," said the Sheriff as he rode up to the victor and presented him with the prize, "what is your name and in what country do you dwell?"

"My name is Reynolde Grenelefe," replied the forester, as he conjured up a name worthy of a marksman. "I was born and bred in merry Holdernesse and am now roving from town to town to seek a better fortune."

"I say!" rejoined the Sheriff, "you are the best archer that ever drew bow in Nottingham. Will you live with me and protect the King's deer from the cursed outlaws?"

"Willingly, and you will pay me well?" answered the forester boldly.

"You will have forty pounds a year and three new suits of clothes and will dine everyday off the King's venison," said the Sheriff.

The artful forester readily agreed, and on the same day took up his abode in his new master's mansion, where he soon became on good terms with all the household, except the steward, who took a mortal aversion to him on account of his favor with their master.

The Sheriff's Pantry

One day the Sheriff went out hunting early in the morning, leaving Reynolde

Grenelefe asleep in bed, where he lay until it was nearly noon. He then rose, and going to the kitchen, asked the steward for his dinner.

"You lazy villain," he replied, "do you think you have earned it. Truthfully you shall have neither food nor drink till my lord hears of your idleness."

The forester laughed and gave a stride towards the pantry door, but the steward was too quick for him. He turned the key in the lock, pulled it out, and placed it in his pocket. Without a word the outlaw stepped up and struck him with his open palm upon the ear, and the poor steward, stunned with the shock, fell heavily down. Reynolde then spurned the door with his foot, bursting lock and bar asunder, and entering the pantry, he found a goodly venison meat pie and a bottle of strong ale, upon which, without either grace or ceremony, he began a most furious attack.

While he was busy the cook came in, and seeing the steward lying on the floor and the new servant devouring the contents of the pantry, he soon guessed the true state of the matter. Arming himself with a huge rolling pin, he crept quietly towards the offender and, before he could protect himself, struck him upon the back of his head. The outlaw well nigh fell, but catching at a board, he sustained himself and then, drawing his sword, rushed at his cowardly antagonist. For full an hour did they thump and belabor each other till they could scarcely stand.

"Give me your hand," cried Reynolde, dropping his sword. "You are a valiant fellow, and it would be a pity to break your bones. Come with me to the woods. I am one of Robin Hood's men, and if you will join us, we'll give you a suit of Lincoln green and teach you the merry life of a forester."

The cook consented and after breaking open their master's treasury and seizing upon all the silver plate and money that it contained, the treacherous servants left the house and, mounting two of the finest horses in the Sheriff's stable, galloped off with their booty to Barnesdale forest.

"Welcome, my brave yeoman. Where have you tarried?" exclaimed Robin Hood, as Little John presented himself and his companion before the gallant captain. "And who do you bring to the greenwood?"

"You will hear all, good master," replied the tall forester. "Your friend, the

Sheriff of Nottingham, has sent you his cook, his silver goblets, and three hundred golden pounds," and he related the story of his adventures with the greatest glee, while Robin Hood, who owed the poor Sheriff many a grudge, laughed till the tears ran down his cheeks, and he was obliged to throw himself upon the grass from sheer exhaustion.

A Curious-Colored Stag

Just as Little John was concluding his narration about his alias, Reynolde, a huntsman's bugle sounded in the distance. He stopped and listened for a moment. "It is the Sheriff of Nottingham's horn," he exclaimed. "I must away to him," and darting through the woods, he ran over hill and dale until he reached the spot where the Sheriff of Nottingham and his attendants were beating among the thickets in search of game.

"Ha! Reynolde Grenelefe," the Sheriff exclaimed, as his servant stood before him, "where have you been?"

"Roving through the forest, good master," replied Reynolde, "and truthfully I have beheld the strangest sight that mortal eyes ever saw. In that dense wood is a fine stag, whose hide is of a bright green color, and a herd of one hundred and forty more lie scattered around him. His horns are so large and sharp that I dare not shoot for fear that he might rush at me and tear me, and hearing your bugle horn, I have hastened to tell you of so strange a creature."

The Sheriff, filled with wonder, desired to be immediately conducted to the animal, and the outlaw started off again at his full speed, followed by the company of men, until they arrived at the spot where Robin Hood was still lying upon the turf. "This is the hare, good master," said Little John, pointing to his captain, "and there is the gallant herd," and he directed the Sheriff's attention to a band of yeomen who were reclining under the shade of some neighboring trees.

"You have betrayed me," he cried, drawing his sword, and biting his lips with rage. "You will suffer for your treachery," and he struck a fierce blow at his conductor.

"Calm you, good master!" exclaimed Little John, nimbly avoiding the weapon. "You have given me many a good dinner, and now you will have a jovial supper in return."

Two foresters advanced and gently disarmed the still threatening prisoner, who very quietly suffered himself to be seated at a well-spread cloth. At the entreaty of the outlaws he began to eat, but when Little John brought him wine in his own silver cup, his mortification was so great that he could not swallow another morsel. The foresters pressed him so much the more and laughed loud and long at his rueful countenance, while two or three sang ballads celebrating their own victory over the Sheriff of Nottingham.

The Sheriff's Couch

The poor man could endure the scene no longer. He started to his feet and would gladly have made his escape, but his flight was arrested. "For one night, Sir Sheriff, you will be an outlaw like us," said Robin Hood to him. "You will have your couch under the green trees of Barnesdale, and if tomorrow you like your fare, we will give you a green mantle and teach you to shoot the grey goose wing."

Night drew on. The foresters, wrapping themselves in their cloaks, laid themselves down under the most shady trees and, binding their prisoner that he might not escape during the darkness, compelled him to share their broad couch. All night long he tossed about and groaned, and when, oppressed with weariness, he at length fell asleep, dreams of the most hideous nature wakened him to fresh torment. The darkness seemed to him interminable, but at length the sun rose, and the foresters one and all roused themselves from their slumbers.

"Have you passed a good night, Sir Sheriff?" asked Robin Hood. "How do you like our downy beds?"

"The beasts of the field lie more softly," replied the Sheriff. "Rather than make me pass another night like this, I pray you send an arrow through my heart, and I'll forgive you. But for what purpose do you detain me? I have no gold, and that traitor Reynolde Grenelefe has robbed me of what I possessed at home. Suffer me to go, and I will be your best friend to my dying day."

"Swear that you will never harm the foresters of Barnesdale," replied Robin Hood, "and you will depart." And he presented the cross of his sword to the Sheriff's lips.

He took the oath, and the outlaw immediately cut his bonds. Then ordering his horse to be brought, he helped the anxious Sheriff to his saddle and bade him a merry ride. The goaded steed flew along the narrow pathway and, quickly emerging from the woods, bore his glad rider home to Nottingham.

A Rural Fair

A twelvemonth was nearly elapsed since Robin Hood had lent the four hundred pounds to the Knight of Wierysdale, and but two days yet remained in the season, when the money would become due.

By economy and service in arms, the Knight had been able to save much more than the required sum. He purchased a hundred tough bows with strings of twisted silk, a hundred beautiful quivers, well stored with arrows—each of which was notched with silver, feathered with the plume of a peacock, and tipped with a head of burnished gold. Mounted on the outlaw's steed, he set out to Barnesdale wood, followed by a troop of his attendants, bearing the weapons of the chase before them.

On his way, the Knight passed through a little town, where the inhabitants were celebrating a rural fair. The banks of a stream, over which he crossed by a rustic wooden bridge, were crowded with gaily-dressed peasants, anxious to purchase the rare commodities, which they were able only once a year to procure at this long-expected fair. There were tents of blue, white, and crimson cloths; and long streaming banners floated proudly above them. There were open stalls too and rich displays of costly goods; and the busy throngs, as they incessantly poured on and on, seemed full of merriment and gladness.

It was a joyous scene, and the Knight gazed upon it with heart-felt pleasure. He wished to join in it, but he remembered that the day was close at hand when he had promised repayment to the generous outlaw, and he struck his spurs into his charger's sides. He had proceeded but a short way when a loud noise broke upon the distant murmur that had hitherto reached him from the meadows and caused him again to draw his rein. It seemed like the quarrelling of men in angry strife, and every moment it grew louder and louder.

"There may be need of our assistance," said the Knight to his followers, and he instantly galloped to the spot whence the confusion arose. At the sight of a band of armed horsemen the crowd became calm and opened a passageway.

"What means this uproar?" asked the leader. "Are you not celebrating games of joy and peace?" A dead silence prevailed. "Tell me, my friend," he continued, addressing one who stood nearest him, "why are you at odds?"

"This stranger," replied the man, pointing to a gallant looking yeoman who rested upon his bow apart from the rest, "has won every prize today. We know him not and think it is unfair that the best men in our county should have no victory."

"Come here, sir," cried the Knight to the offender. "Who are you that dares to shoot and wrestle better than any man in Nottinghamshire?"

The yeoman stepped forward boldly. "What can it matter, Sir Knight, who I am?" he replied. "I've won the prizes and have a right to them, but these poor clowns cannot stomach a heavy fall or my arrow in the center of their bull's eyes."

"Shame on you, my friends. Would you wrong a victor of his lawful reward?" exclaimed the Knight, turning to the multitude. "Where are the prizes?"

An old man advanced and, taking the horseman's bridle, led him to a tent, where were spread upon the grass a handsome saddle and bridle, ornamented with gold, the prize of the swiftest runner; a finely carved bow, and an arrow, three feet long, of the purest white silver, to be given to the truest marksman; and a pipe of the best Rhenish wine to be awarded to him who should gain the day at wrestling. All these had the stranger indubitably won, but when he demanded them, the disappointment of the native peasants broke out into loud murmurings, and as few espoused the cause of the victor, it had well nigh gone hard with him. Staves had been brought into play, and more than one sword had been drawn, when the arrival of the knight and his attendants quieted the tumult.

"Have you a steed to bear this goodly saddle?" said the Knight to the stranger, "and how will you carry off this pipe of wine?"

"I came on foot," replied the man, "but rather than leave so brave a prize, I will bear the saddle on my own back. As for the cask, these good peasants are

welcome to it."

"You are a noble fellow," returned the Knight of Wierysdale, throwing him a purse of gold. "There's for your wine, and if you will follow me, you will have a charger for your saddle."

The yeoman readily complied. One of the Knight's men dismounted, and gave up his horse to him. He quickly clapped on his elegant accouterments, and with the bow at his back and quiver by his side, he sprang into the seat and arranged himself with the rest of the attendants. The aristocratic liaison next ordered that the wine should be broached and distributed to all who would partake of it. The command was quickly obeyed, amidst the cheers of the peasants, who soon forgot their previous quarrels and disappointments in the pleasures of the jovial cup. The Knight waved his hand to them and rode on, but he had lost so much time at the fair, that the sun sank down long before he reached the woods of Barnesdale, and he was obliged to halt at a little cottage by the wayside.

The next day was the annual celebration of the year's harvest. Robin Hood ordered a fat buck to be dressed and preparations made for his expected guest. Ladies Marian and Cristabel added to the feast and looked forward to serving its fare to their honored guest; but noon passed without any appearance of him.

"Go you," said the outlaw to his favorite attendant, "and see if you can spy this slothful Knight. Take Will Scarlet and the Miller's Son with you."

"Take care, my Robin," said Marian, "for we do not know the reason for his absence. Perchance he has fallen into danger."

Robin agreed and turning to Little John said, "If his faithful surety sends any over-burdened travelers to pay my debt, bring them hither. But, I charge you, if a poor man or a merry jester or a damsel in distress pass by, help them to your utmost, give them gold and assist them on their way."

The Monks of St. Mary's Abbey

The three foresters gladly obeyed and soon reached the high road that ran through the wood. Many a stout yeoman and honest peasant did they encounter and pass with a fair salutation, and one poor beggar, half clothed in rags, was sent on his path rejoicing. As they reached the summit of a hill, two monks riding upon horses, attended by about a score of armed men on foot and six pack mules heavily laden, appeared just ascending upon the opposite side.

"I'll wager my best bowstring," exclaimed Little John, "that these reverend fathers have brought our captain's money. Bend your bows, my lads, and scatter the herd that follows them."

The foresters let fly arrow after arrow in such quick succession that the frightened travelers turned and fled precipitately; the archers pursued and soon gained upon the fugitives, who one and all rushed into the woods and endeavored to escape amid the concealment of the foliage. Those on foot soon disappeared, but the two monks on their horses and the pack mules were easily captured by the outlaws. They immediately tied the hands of their prisoners behind them and, fastening the reins of their steeds together, they drove them to the presence of the chief, who tipped his cap and advanced with great courtesy to meet his guests.

"I pray you, Reverend Fathers," he said to them, "take no offence at the rough treatment of my followers. I care not to dine unless in good company, and therefore did they bring you from your straight journeying." The monks preserved a sullen silence and suffered their bonds to be cut, and they dismounted without speaking a word.

"Mercy, good sirs," cried Robin Hood, "I think you have but a small share of courtesy. What abbey do you inhabit?"

"We are but poor brethren of St. Mary's Abbey," replied one of the monks, who was the high cellarer and therefore responsible for the provisions of food and drink at the Abbey, "and are on our way to London to pay reverence to the Pope's representative, who has required our presence."

"May his blessing attend you," said the outlaw, in a mock solemn tone. "Come now, my good friends, the feast is spread. Sit you and make merry."

It is probable that in their present condition the monks would have declined this request had not the savory odor that arose from a smoking haunch of venison and a roasted wild swan smoothed down their angry feelings. They were soon seated by the side of the gallant forester. The monks ate heartily and quaffed many a cup to their host and his merry men, forgetting, in their enjoyment, that they would pay dearly for the treat. Robin Hood laughed and sang, and his men trolled out their legendary ballads until the sun had nearly reached the horizon.

"I fear me," said the outlaw to Little John, "that God is upset with us. The day is well nigh spent, and our four hundred pounds are yet to come."

"Never fear," replied the tall forester. These kind monks have brought it, I dare say, for they come from the abbey. Tell us, good Fathers, have you not repayment for us from your abbey?"

"We have heard naught of this before," replied the high cellarer. "We possess but twenty marks to defray the expenses of our travelling. Let us be on our way, kind sirs, or we will never reach Nottingham this night."

"If you have but twenty marks," returned Robin Hood, "you will have to beg for charity before you reach your journey's end. See, my bold Little John, how much you can find in those heavy looking trunks. If it is as you say I will charge you nothing for your feast, but if you have a prize, you must even be content to part with it."

Little John soon returned with the trunk upon his shoulders, and spreading his mantle upon the grass, he poured out a heap of gold upon it.

"Good master, here are eight hundred pounds or more," he said, "Truthfully you could not have wished for better payment."

The monks' vexation was now at its height. They bit their lips and cast anxious glances towards their riding horses.

"You will need some few of these," said Robin Hood, as he gave a handful of gold pieces to each of them. "The patron of your abbey has sent us the rest as repayment for the money we lent to the Knight of Wierysdale." They eagerly clutched the offered gold and, without opposition from the outlaws, mounted their steeds with most surprising quickness and, leaving the pack mules behind them, rode off amid loud shouts of laughter.

The topmost branches of the trees alone were gilded with the rays of the setting sun, and the foliage had begun to cast a deeper shade, when a party of horsemen emerged from the woods upon the lawn where the bold foresters were merrily regaling themselves at the expense of the poor monks whom they had plundered.

In an instant they started to their feet, and fifty shafts were leveled at the intruders. But when the foremost rider leaped from his horse and threw himself into the arms of Robin Hood, they easily recognized him as Sir Richard of the Lee.

"Welcome, Sir Knight, thrice welcome!" exclaimed the outlaw. "Truly you look more merry than when last I saw you in these woods. Have you recovered your fair domains?"

"Ten thousand thanks to you, my noble, my generous friend!" cried the Knight. "I still hold my father's lands, and with the blessing of God, I am come to return the sum I borrowed of you."

"It is already paid, my gallant sir," returned Robin Hood. "Two monks from the St. Mary's Abbey have this day brought me back my gold with interest, so keep your money, and when you see a man in need, remember Robin Hood."

The Knight's Gratitude

"Truly, you will overwhelm me with your kindness," replied the Knight. "I would have been with you before noon, but that knave you see there had the audacity to win every prize at a village festival, and had I not interceded, he would have received a sorry recompense for his achievements."

"Ha! Have you one of my truest men among your followers?" exclaimed the outlaw, as he recognized the victor. "George of the Green would have stood toughly against a score of peasants, I think."

"Yes, good master," joined in the forester, "but what can one arm do against sixty? Truthfully, I should have had a morning bath, if it had not been for this gallant knight."

Robin Hood whispered a few words to Little John, who left them and almost instantly returned with a bag of gold.

"Take this, good Sir," said the chief outlaw, as he handed it to the Knight. "The monks of St. Mary's paid me too much by four hundred pounds. You cannot yet be rich. Take it as a reward for your generous intercession."

The Knight would have refused the gold, but he knew that by so doing he should displease his generous friend. "I accept your gift," he replied. "One day I may be able to repay your goodness. Until then I will remain in your debt. But I entreat you, receive this poor present as a humble tribute of my gratitude." At his command, his followers alighted from their steeds and laid the bows and quivers at the outlaw's feet.

The foresters all shouted for joy as their chief distributed the handsome gifts among them. Many started off at once to try their new weapons, while the others, resuming their seats upon the grass, helped the Knight and his followers with unbounded liberality and passed the rest of the evening in drinking and singing till darkness closed upon their gaiety. Couches of fern and dried rushes were prepared for the guests, who slept soundly in the foresters' rude bowers until the bugle horn wakened them from their dreams at the dawn of morning. The Knight, anxious to return to his lady and children, stayed not for breakfast. Bidding farewell to the kind outlaws, he sprung into his horse's saddle and, with his attendants, rode off to his beloved home in Wierysdale.

VI

OUR LAST EVENING
AMONG SCHOOL FELLOWS

My legends of Robin Hood were nearly exhausted. The midsummer holidays were drawing near and we should soon be busily engaged in striving for the prizes that were awarded to the most proficient scholars.

"This is the last time I will tell you of bold Robin Hood," said I, when my schoolfellows had gathered round me. "But if, after the holidays are passed, we all meet again, I will endeavor to find some other bygone stories to relate to you that I hope will be equally interesting." They thanked me warmly, and I continued.

The Sheriff's Complaint

When the monks of St. Mary's Abbey had escaped from the hands of the outlaws, they urged on their steeds to the utmost. They did not draw rein until they reached the good town of Nottingham. Without delay, they sought the Sheriff of the county, and made known to him the treatment they had received in the woods of Barnesdale.

That worthy official listened with great attention to their complaint, and still burning with revenge for the many insults that he had received from the outlaws, promised that he would rest neither night nor day till Robin Hood and his men were taken. Not knowing exactly how to accomplish this, he determined to lay the matter before the King. Mounting his fleetest steed, he rode with great haste to London, where he demanded an audience of the valiant monarch, who had just returned from his long captivity in the castle at Dürnstein, Austria.

"What!" cried King Richard, when the Sheriff had finished his complaint. "Can you not take a sorry rebel who owns not a single castle? You are a coward! If you do not bring me that outlaw's head within half a year, your position will be given to a better man."

The Golden Arrow

The poor Sheriff felt his disgrace and returned slowly home to Nottingham, pondering on the King's words, and devising plans by which he might retrieve his lost standing with the King. He thought of a notable scheme. He proclaimed that an archery meeting would be held at Nottingham and that a golden arrow would be given to the victor of the games.

The day arrived, but he in vain looked for the coats of Lincoln green that he had hoped would be among the crowd, and he rode about anxiously endeavoring to discover the outlaws of Sherwood. There were gallant yeomen in mantles of blue, buff, and scarlet, and some there were in green, but they were good bowmen of Nottingham, and the Sheriff was almost in despair. He ordered the sports to commence, and never was better archery shown before.

A tall stranger with a light blue jacket excited the admiration of everyone, and the arrow would have been his prize, but a rival yeoman followed and shot with such dexterity that he fairly eclipsed all those who had preceded him. He was dressed in a bright scarlet coat, crossed by a silken belt, from which was suspended a little bugle horn of silver and gold; his lower limbs were clothed in the skin of a deer, bleached as white as snow; and upon his head he wore a long black hood, which fell gracefully down his back.

When the sports were concluded, this merry forester was unanimously declared the winner of the day, and amid the shouts of the spectators, he was led to the tent beneath which the Sheriff of Nottingham stood to award the golden arrow. The stranger fell upon one knee, and with much praise of his gallant archery, the prize was delivered to him. He rose, placed the arrow in his belt, and a triumphant smile lighted up his features as, for one moment, he looked at the Sheriiff's face. It was enough; the Sheriff caught the glance, and it acted like magic upon him.

"Ho! Guards, seize him!" he shouted with his utmost strength. "It's Robin Hood, the outlawed rebel! Five hundred pounds for his head!"

In a second, the forester had gained the middle of the field and had blown a long shrill blast upon his horn. At the signal, yeomen flew from every part of the field and arranged themselves around him. The Sheriff was astounded. He cried to his men to follow; and mounting his horse, he galloped towards the daring rebels. A flight of arrows met him half way, and his steed fell tumbling to the earth. The rider arose unharmed, but his men had fled on all sides, and he was obliged to follow them.

"Base cowards," he cried, "you will be hung on the highest gallows in Nottingham." Snatching a huge crossbow from the hands of one of the fugitives, he leveled it at the retreating band and fired. One man dropped. It was the tall forester in the light blue coat.

A Desperate Combat

At this, the Sheriff's followers took courage and with a loud shout, dashed onwards in pursuit of the outlaws, who had taken up their wounded companion and were now full half a mile in advance. Arrows innumerable fell like hailstones on each party, and many of the Nottingham men fell, sorely hurt. The chase continued, and the Sheriff seemed still determined to pursue. For hours did the foresters use their fleetest speed, turning ever and again to discharge their bows, until they were well nigh exhausted. They would have stopped and fought, but the overwhelming numbers that pursued gave them but a poor chance of victory.

In this extremity, a young knight, riding upon a grey charger and attended by several armed horsemen, met them upon the road. Surprised at so unusual a sight, the knight reined up his steed and disposed his men around him as if to challenge the road. This bold step had well nigh proven his ruin. A hundred arrows were pointed at him and, at a word, would have pierced through his breastplate to his heart.

"Hold," shouted Robin Hood, dropping his bow. "It is Sir Richard of the Lee! It is the good Knight of Wierysdale." The Knight recognized the voice and a few words briefly explained to him the reason for their flight.

Wierysdale Castle

"To my castle, to my castle!" he cried. "It is close at hand and will defy the Sheriff of Nottingham with ten thousand of his men." Then vaulting into his saddle, he took the wounded forester, Little John, before him upon his steed, pointed out his fortress to Robin Hood, and galloped away.

The castle of Wierysdale, surrounded on every side by stately trees, stood upon a slight eminence in the middle of an extensive valley. The building itself was of immense strength. It was girded by a lofty stone wall, six feet in thickness, and two ditches of considerable breadth and depth encompassed it. Over these were bridges that could be raised or lowered at pleasure, and a strong iron door was the only way of entrance to the castle.

The outlaws increased their speed and soon reached this promised refuge. The gates were wide open. They rushed in, and at a word the drawbridges were raised, and the iron gates dropped. In a few more minutes the Sheriff, with his followers at his heels, loudly demanded admittance. "Sir traitor Knight," he cried, "you are aiding the enemy of the King! If you do not deliver up the outlaws of Sherwood you will be branded as a traitor."

"Away, proud braggart," retorted the Knight. "Do you threaten me? By my good sword you will one day regret your insolence. I will avow the deed that I have done, even to the loss of my lands. Go now to the King and learn what is his will in this matter. Till then Robin Hood and his men are safe with me."

A flight of arrows stopped further talks, and the Sheriff was in despair. It was useless for the Sheriff, even with the multitude that he had at his command, to attempt forcing the castle, and the Knight had set his authority at defiance. Burning with disappointment and rage, he denounced him as a traitor to his King, and rushing through the mass that crowded behind him, he returned to Nottingham then to London to tell the tale to the King.

"As crowned King and belted Knight," said Richard the Lionheart, "but these fellows hold together truly and stanchly! The more I hear of them, the greater grows my wish to see them. Go back, Sheriff, and stir no more in this matter at present. I myself will come to Nottingham shortly and look into these things myself."

The Sheriff had been hoping to get orders from the King to raise the whole country on Sir Richard's castle, and so he was greatly disappointed. There was nothing for him to do but go home defeated and wait for the King, while Sir Richard of the Lea feasted Robin Hood and his foresters upon the most delicate food, such as they seldom met in their forest retreats. The Knight's lady nursed Little John's wound, which quickly healed; and before long, he winded his bugle horn as merry as the rest among the echoing woods of Barnesdale. In their brief stay at the castle of Wierysdale under the care of Sir Richard and his wife, Robin Hood and his men rested and regained health and strength.

The Sheriff's Capture of Sir Richard

The defeated Sheriff neither forgot nor forgave the treatment that he had received. He was determined upon seeking revenge on the rebellious Knight and set spies around his castle to give him intelligence when he departed from it. For a long time they watched in vain, but one summer's morning the Knight and his lady rode out to amuse themselves in the delightful sport of falconry. Their steeds bounded gaily along the meadows by the banks of a river, and they rode far away from home. A solitary heron that had been patiently watching for fish in a shallow part of the stream, frightened at their approach, rose with a shrill scream and soared high up in air. The lady checked her horse, untied the leash strap that confined a falcon to her wrist, and threw it off.

The bird flew upwards as if shot from a bow and rapidly ascended higher than the quarry. Fluttering its wings, it hovered for an instant above and, shooting downwards, struck the heron with its sharp beak and bore it to the earth. The lady was delighted and, applying a silver whistle to her mouth, recalled the well-trained hawk, which flew back again to her hand.

Pleased with the sport, they galloped over many a verdant plain and flowery mead, and noon was long past before they thought of returning. They were conversing about Robin Hood and his bold foresters and wondering why they had heard nothing more of the Sheriff of Nottingham, when they became aware of six armed horsemen galloping towards them at their utmost speed. Little imagining their intentions, the Knight quietly pursued his course, when, to his surprise, the men checked their steeds as they approached, and with drawn swords in their hands, they surrounded him. In the leader, the unfortunate Knight easily recognized the Sheriff of Nottingham, and he guessed his fate. The good Knight was fastened with a plaited leather cord to his saddle, his arms were tied behind his back, and he was led away captive.

His lady, aware that resistance was fruitless, turned her horse's head and galloped swiftly from the spot. Full of courage for her gallant husband, she rode on without drawing rein until she reached the forest of Sherwood, into which she fearlessly entered. A youth was lying upon the grass under a broad tree. "My friend," she cried to him, "can you tell me where to find bold Robin Hood?"

The young man came to his feet and tipping his cap, replied, "I am one of Robin Hood's foresters, gracious lady, and will conduct you to him." Taking the horse's rein in his hand, he led it through the narrow paths to the spot where the bold outlaw was shading himself from the summer's heat beneath a rustic bower.

"God save you, good Robin Hood," said the lady as the forester advanced. "Grant me your aid and quickly. Your enemy, the Sheriff, has bound my husband and led him captive to Nottingham."

The outlaw replied by setting his bugle horn to his lips and sounding a shrill blast. It was answered from every side and one hundred forty men soon gathered around him.

"Hurry, my merry men," he cried to them, "to the rescue of the Knight of Wierysdale. That double villain, the Sheriff of Nottingham, has captured him. He that will not fight for our good friend is no longer follower of mine. And you, my lady, stay with my wife Marian and Lady Cristabel here in the greenwood until such time that we return with your Knight in shining armor.

You will be safe and in good company."

The Return of the Knight of Wierysdale

The men gave a loud shout to prove their readiness, and their captain, bidding the lady to be of good cheer and await the issue back home in her castle, darted through the woods. The foresters followed him in a crowd close upon his heels. Neither hedge nor stream stopped their progress. They leaped over every obstacle and in two hours reached the town of Nottingham. They were just in time. The jailer was even at the moment unbarring the gates of the castle to admit the prisoner, and the Sheriff was unfastening the bonds by which he was held to his horse.

At the appearance of the outlaws, the astonished inhabitants raised a loud cry, and the Sheriff leaped into his saddle. He had but a small force at hand, quite insufficient to oppose the assailants, and seizing his prisoner's bridle rein, he attempted to flee. It was too late. An arrow from the bow of the foremost outlaw pierced through the Sheriff's shoulder, and he fell headlong from his steed. His attendants were routed, and the Knight of Wierysdale was recaptured. Robin Hood himself cut his bonds with a dagger, and raised a loud shout of victory.

He and his gallant foresters retired to merry Sherwood where the Knight was reunited with his lady and given hospitable care by Ladies Marian and Christabel. Upon the morrow, they all went to Wierysdale; the Knight and his lady showed them warm thanks in the form of a glorious feast, after which they returned to their customary abodes in the greenwood.

The Outlaw's Allegiance and Pardon

The excitement caused by the defeat of the Sheriff of Nottingham was not easily appeased. Intelligence of the outrage was carried to King Richard, who had recently returned to England. He summoned a council to devise the best means of putting down the fearless rebels. They declared the Knight of Wierysdale an outlaw, and his lands, which were forfeited to the crown, were offered as a reward to whomsoever should take the traitor, Robin Hood, dead or alive. Fifty knights volunteered their services, and Sherwood Forest became too hot for the brave outlaws, who retired by stealth to Plompton Park in Cumberland, where they concealed themselves for many weeks. At last, receiving intelligence that the search was abandoned, they ventured to return to Sherwood.

After a time King Richard came down to Nottingham in hopes of meeting with Robin Hood. He marched into the forest attended by a strong body of knights and expected to encounter the outlaws very shortly. But he marched hither and thither and found the forest empty and silent as far as all human life was concerned; he saw the deer bounding over the greensward, the great oaks waving their boughs in the wind, but never a glimpse had he of the stout fellows in Lincoln green.

Day after day passed, and Richard traversed the glade and woodland all in vain; he seemed no nearer to coming to speech with Robin Hood than he had been when seated in his palace in London. "By my word," said King Richard, "but this is strange. I was told that these fellows so haunted the forest roads that a beggar could not pass unnoticed, and yet I see naught of them."

The reason was simple: it was Robin's own doing that Richard saw nothing of the outlaws. Robin loved his King and was not willing that a hand should be raised against Richard and his followers, so he gave strict orders that his men should keep out of the way.

He was faithfully obeyed. Time and again the outlaws lay hidden in brush and thicket as the glittering train swept by and smiled to see the King and his lords pass within easy bowshot, but never an arrow was placed on string, and never a sign was given of their presence.

One day Richard was lamenting that Robin Hood seemed to have vanished from the face of the earth when an old forester who stood by his knee smiled and said, "Nay, my liege Lord, he is in the forest as surely as I stand here, and you may easily see him."

"How?" demanded the King.

"Why, my Lord, you go in armor and with a train of soldiery. Think you that the outlaws will set green jacket against coat of mail armor? I think not. But should you go in guise of an abbot, whose mails would yield rich plunder on rifling, I warrant me that Robin would appear fast enough."

King Richard saw the force of these words and nodded gaily. The adventure was just to his liking, and the very next day, he slipped secretly from Nottingham in abbot's dress, with half a dozen followers dressed as monks and extra horses that were led along, heavily laden with stores and baggage.

Sure enough, he had not gone three miles into the forest before he was called upon to stand. At a bend of the way, he interrupted Robin and his men, advancing towards them, riding upon steeds richly decorated. Robin looked at the entourage of monks. The foremost was a man of most commanding presence. He was of noble countenance, tall stature, well proportioned, and apparently of Herculean strength. As he sat upright upon his saddle and glanced around him, his stately expression but ill accorded with the peaceful character of the white robe that covered him. Robin Hood knew him not and wondered what bold bishop it could be who had ventured to enter upon the proscribed domains.

"By your leave, Sir Abbot," Robin cried, as he stepped from a thicket and laid his hand upon the horse's bridle, "you must abide a while. If you have gold in your purse, by the laws of Sherwood Forest it is forfeited."

"And who are you who bars my way?" asked the foremost bishop in his deep, rich voice.

Robin Hood started slightly at hearing those commanding tones and looked keenly at the stranger. "We are yeomen of this forest. We dwell beneath the greenwood tree, and we live on our King's deer, for we have no other means. But you have churches, rents, and much gold; give us of your plenty, for charity's sake."

"Good yeoman," replied the Bishop, "in truth I have but forty pounds. King Richard has been at Nottingham, and the merry follies of the court have swallowed up the rest." Drawing a purse from his girdle, he gave it to the outlaw, who counted out the bright gold pieces into his hand.

"You will need these, perchance," he said, as he gave back half the money.

"We may meet again and you canst then repay me."

"Mercy, but you are a gentle thief," exclaimed the Bishop. "If, as I strongly suspect, you are bold Robin Hood, Richard, King of England, sends you his signet by me and bids you come to him in the good town of Nottingham." He drew the royal signet from beneath his cloak and showed it.

The outlaw bent his knee in respect as he beheld the royal signet, and every yeoman pulled off his hood and stood bareheaded.

"Why," said the Bishop in surprise, "I was told, yeoman, that you were a disloyal fellow who set the King's law at naught and did all kinds of evil."

"Nay, Sir Abbot," replied Robin. "I hate unjust sheriffs and greedy monks, but I love no man in all the world so well as I do my gallant King, and if you are his messenger and bear his signet, I will obey your request. I can trust to the honor of King Richard and for love of him, Sir Bishop. But first I make you welcome to the greenwood, and today you shall dine with me under my meeting tree for the love our King."

Robin put wind to his bugle horn merrily and made the old trees echo with the blast. To the King's great astonishment, it was replied to, and one hundred forty men bounded to the summons. Richard was struck and thought, "These fellows are more at his bidding than my men be at mine. The stories I hear of Robin Hood are true."

A cloth was spread upon the grass and plentifully supplied with venison, fowls, fish, cans of fine brown ale, and bowls of ruby wine. The disguised Bishop and his companions seated themselves, and a jovial feast ensued. "Let us drink to the health of King Richard," cried the outlaw, filling his goblet to the brim. "He who fails me in this pledge is no friend of Robin Hood's." They ate and drank and enjoyed the abundant fare of the greenwood to the full.

Loud cries of "Long live the King," rose from all sides, and in imitation of their host, each man emptied his cup and reversed it upon the cloth before him.

"Bend your bows, my gallant followers," said the outlaw, "and show our guests the archery of Sherwood." A willow wand was fixed in the earth at a long distance off, and a garland of wild roses was suspended upon its top. The laws of the game were that whoever missed the garland should lose his bow and arrows and receive a strike upon his bare head. One by one the foresters advanced and all shot true, until Little John carelessly missed the wand by three good inches. Robin Hood gave him a blow upon his ear that made it ring for many an after hour and then took his own turn. To his great dismay his shaft flew on the outer side of the garland.

His men shouted with laughter. "You have lost your bow, good master!" they cried in the greatest glee. "The Bishop will give you your pay." The Priest laughed too and turning up the sleeves of his gown stepped toward the outlaw.

Robin Hood stood firm and folded his arms upon his breast, but the stalwart Bishop bestowed such a buffet upon his head that he rolled over and over upon the grass.

"Truthfully," cried he, when he had recovered his feet, "there is substance in that arm of yours. I'll warrant me you can shoot a bow as well as we can." The Bishop laughed again and taking up Robin Hood's forfeited weapon, let fly at the garland. The arrow, strongly shot, flew above the wand and struck into a tree on the further side of the lawn.

"Now you must take your pay," exclaimed the outlaw, and striding towards him, he gave him a vigorous blow, but the Priest did not waver an inch.

At that instant a horseman galloped swiftly across the plain and, leaping from his steed, ran to them. It was the Knight of Wierysdale. "Away, my brave men, away," he shouted, "King Richard is seeking for you. The forest is beset with men, and you will…." He suddenly paused. His eye had caught the keen glance with which the Bishop was regarding him. He threw himself at his feet. "Pardon, gracious Sire," he exclaimed, "one who has served you long and faithfully."

Robin Hood was struck dumb; the truth flashed across his mind. It was King Richard whom he had so unceremoniously buffeted! He fell upon his knees by the Knight's side and sued for mercy. His men also in like manner bowed before their sovereign.

"With such audience as witnesses this day, I make two proclamations," exclaimed the King. "Sir Knight, you have done wrong, but I forgive you. Rise, your lands are restored to you. As for you, you valiant traitor," he continued, placing his hand on Robin Hood's head, "on one condition only can

I grant your pardon. You and your men must be my royal archers of Sherwood. Together you shall protect all travelers from thieves and harm. In exchange you may roam freely through these great woods of Sherwood with all rights to my game; my deer are your deer, and my forest is your forest."

Robin rose and humbly received the King's offer. Robin Hood was acknowledged as the official leader of his forest band. The outlaws shouted with rapture, flinging their hats in the air. Cries of "Long live King Richard" filled the air and every man bent his knee to their royal master. With their acceptance of his offer, the King appointed Robin Hood as Earl of Sherwood and gave a place of dignity to both Little John and Will Scarlet.

Later that day, such excitement there was, when it became known that Robin and his men were marching in a body to the town, shouting and singing as they came. Some people were frightened and wanted to run away, but they did not know where to run. Everybody wanted to see the sight. They came out of their houses and stood in the streets or leaned from the windows, all anxious to see what was happening.

"They have killed the King," some said.

"They are coming to take the town."

"They mean to hang the Sheriff."

"And the Normans too!"

"They are going to beat all the monks and friars!"

"They will pull the monastery down."

The excitement grew and grew, till everyone's face was red and every throat was hoarse.

"They have not killed the King at all," someone shouted at last. "Look! He is riding at the head of them along with Robin Hood. Long live King Richard. Long live Robin Hood. Hurrah! Hurrah!"

> *The King soon let them understand*
> *He had been in the greenwood;*
> *And on that day, and forevermore,*
> *Had forgiven the outlaw Robin Hood.*

There was great rejoicing when the people heard that Robin Hood and the King were comrades. They walked up and down the streets nearly all day, singing "God save the King."

The only person who was sorry was the Sheriff. "What! Robin Hood," said he, "that creature whom I hate?"

But Robin Hood came to him and said, "I have brought you back the money you paid me for your dinner in the forest."

The Sheriff was delighted to get his three hundred pounds again. He was so glad that he almost forgave Robin for all the mischief he had caused.

"Now," said Robin laughing. "I have given you back your money, so you owe me a dinner for that one I gave you in the forest. Ask the King if he will honor you by coming to supper. If he does, I will come too."

The Sheriff groaned. "If I ask the King to supper it will cost me three hundred pounds and more."

"Of course it will," replied Robin. "See that it is a fine supper, and worthy of a King."

So the poor Sheriff was obliged to ask the King to supper. He came, and so did Robin Hood and his own entourage of merry men. It was a very fine supper indeed. But the poor Sheriff could hardly eat anything. It made him miserable to see the King and his old enemy Robin Hood so amicable. And the thought of all the money he had spent made him more miserable still.

The next day, the King and his entourage mounted their horses and retired to London. In the weeks and months that followed, Robin Hood breathed the delightful air of Sherwood and ranged through many a well-known thicket and often frequented lawn. But Richard did not stay in England long, for he soon returned to France to deal with King Philip II. And not long thereafter, unfortunately, Richard Cœur de Lion was killed. Since he had no sons, his brother, Prince John, became King of England.

Now Prince John hated Robin, so once more he had to fly to the greenwood of Sherwood with all his merry men. The brave hero and his beloved wife Marian lived the rest of their many days in the merry woods of Sherwood.

Long after Robin Hood's time on earth had passed, his fame lived on. Age after age and generation after generation, his memory lingered among the common people who loved to recall his famous exploits and the doings of his great followers. Kings and nobles' deeds were recorded in musty books of record. But minstrels and rhymers made ballad after ballad of the doings of Robin Hood, and these ballads live on the lips and in the hearts of the people. They were sung or recited on holidays and at merry makings, and no rhymes were so popular as those which told of this English hero—a protector of the poor, a foe to the tyrant, brave, gentle, and chivalrous.

Tradition says a stone was set up where he was buried, and on it was graven the inscription:

> *Here, underneath this little stone,*
> *Lies Robert, our Robin, all alone;*
> *Ne'er archer as he was so good,*
> *And people called him "Robin Hood."*
> *Such outlaws as he and his men,*
> *Will England never see again.*

I was obliged to hurry the latter part of my stories more than I could have wished, but I had scarcely finished before our faithful monitor, the sonorous school bell, called us to our less adventuresome but more important pursuits.

The holidays soon after commenced, and we all returned home.

VII

A REUNION OF SCHOOLFELLOWS
AT THE MEETING TREE

Having ended our holidays and returned to school, my schoolfellows longed for more stories. Robin Hood was still on their minds, and they wished to hear of more adventure. So we trod our well-beaten path to the old sycamore tree, our meeting place, and found its weather-beaten trunk and low limbs waiting for us. Wanting to give Robin Hood a legacy linked to modern times, I recounted a tale of history that was as ever full of wonder and intrigue as any tale of Robin.

Though Robin Hood was known as an outlaw by breaking the law, it was because he wanted to right injustices he saw. And though he thought that the end justified the means, what he did, or rather what those from whom his story is based did, led to the formation of one of the most celebrated documents in history. Of course, our Robin Hood is a folk hero, but the real likes of him changed the English-speaking world forever. It is an amazing story, so listen well.

Magna Carta

In a room in The British Library in London, where all may see, rests a manuscript. Though battered, discolored, shriveled with age, and damaged by fire, it is dear to the heart not merely of every Englishman but of every lover of human freedom the world over. It is called Magna Carta, which is Latin for The Great Charter. From it still hangs the royal seal, token of the covenant wrung hundreds of years ago from the reluctant hands of the most cruel and

treacherous of England's kings, King John. It is the parent of countless charters of human freedom. Because of it and of what grew out of it years later, all countries where the English tongue is spoken, and many others as well, enjoy rights of free speech, free parliaments, trial by jury, and liberty.

Imagine that we are back in the days of early June, 1215 and are sailing up the River Thames in a boat from London. Eight hundred years ago, London did not look much like the huge city of today. It was a town of about forty thousand inhabitants, built along the north bank of the Thames River, somewhat in the shape of a bow. The great defensive wall that the Romans had built around AD 200, with seven double gates, was still standing, though rapidly falling into decay. The streets were very narrow, and the upper parts of the houses were built out over the lower stories, so you could almost shake hands with your neighbor on the other side of the lane.

As we leave the old town behind us—for even in those remote days London was an ancient city—and turn our boat up the Thames, we see on every side the homes of the London merchants, with their gardens and orchards, and here and there the castle of one of the great nobles, surrounded by splendid parks. On the river itself, barges float quietly, in search of business or pleasure; graceful swans glide along the banks; and here and there a fish leaps from the water and disappears again. Further upstream, the city and its suburbs are lost to sight, and the dense forest comes down to the water's edge. Presently we come to a small town, then to another.

At last we see the buildings of the town of Staines on the north bank of the river. Here there is tremendous anticipation, for this is the headquarters of the revolting barons who are in league against the King. Nobles and knights, clad in armor and mounted on fiery chargers, along with their men-at-arms, are about to embark for the place of meeting.

Some miles beyond Staines, on the opposite side of the river, standing on the brow of a hill overlooking the Thames, we see presently the towers and turrets and battlements of the royal palace of Windsor, from the gates of which King John and his courtiers, with those few nobles who have still remained true to his cause, are even now riding forth to meet the barons.

The meeting place is a beautiful but boggy meadow on the margin of the river, known even to this day as Runnymede. It is about midway between Staines and Windsor. Long before the days of King John it had been celebrated as a place where the Saxon people were accustomed to meet together under an ancient yew tree to talk over the affairs of the nation. The selection of a muddy bog between Windsor Castle, from where the King ruled, and Staines, the base for the rebel barons, was a neutral site to prevent potential military conflict.

Let us leave our boat and watch the spectacle. A throne has been set up for the King; near it is a regal tent, above which flies the royal standard of England, and round about are the lesser tents of the nobles and courtiers. On the opposite side of the river is the camp of the barons who are forcing the haughty King John, master of arbitrary power and perpetuator of excessive taxation, to capitulate to their terms. Despite years of peace negotiations, King John continues to ignore the requests of the feudal barons for reform and pursues heavy taxation of them to finance his foreign wars. He dares resist the barons no longer, for they have organized a military faction and captured London. He must submit, knowing his country and his kingship are at stake.

Presently the rebel barons cross the river with their squires and men-at-arms, all armed in case the King should contemplate any treachery. The King, who has summoned all of the royal regalia and symbols of his power and office, proceeds from his tent and mounts the throne. He wears his royal robes, glistening with precious stones; a golden, sparkling crown is on his head; and although he makes a royal impression, there is a cruel and crafty smile upon his lips. Beside the King stands the venerable Archbishop of Canterbury, Stephen Langton, who is one of the most scholarly and wise men in England and the negotiator between the two opposing parties.

The barons now stand before King John, led by Robert Fitzwalter, whom they had some time before elected as their leader, Marshal of the Army of God and Holy Church. Each of the barons and knights is dressed in glittering chain armor, with his trusted sword buckled to his side, prepared to fight if necessary. The rebels present King John with their demands for reform, the Articles of the Barons. With the pragmatic mediation of Archbishop Langton between the two factions, a charter capturing the peace agreement is produced.

The Charter of English Liberties, subsequently known as Magna Carta, is brought forth and read to the King on June 15, 1215. On June 19, 1215, the rebel barons make peace with King John and formally renew their oaths of allegiance to him. Magna Carta addresses the baronial complaints but also forms a wider proposal for political reform. It promises the protection of church rights, access to swift justice, protection from illegal imprisonment, and limitations on taxation.

The Forest Charter

Less well known but as significant as Magna Carta is Carta de Foresta, Latin for the Charter of the Forest. An offspring of Magna Carta, it was issued the same year that Magna Carta was reissued for a second time in 1217. Magna Carta was given its official name to distinguish it from this Forest Charter. The Forest Charter expanded three sections of Magna Carta that dealt specifically with the Royal Forests.

The Forest Charter and The Great Charter are companion charters, because both affected the rule of law and forest liberties. The stories of Robin Hood are set in a time when the rights of forest use were contested. The King had the "right of venison," and his subjects had the "right of vert" (forest produce such as herbs, berries, timber). These "greenwoods" were rich in vegetation and wildlife, so the question of who had rights to them was central to the conflicts between the throne and the royal subjects. Robin Hood's story is about these disputes of forest rights. Sherwood Forest was indeed one of the Royal Forests and therefore an appropriate setting for Robin Hood's adventures.

By 1225, when Magna Carta was reissued for the third time, it was well established that the King was not above the law, which is still held today. The famous professor of English law, William Blackstone, republished the Forest Charter and The Great Charter in 1759, making them accessible to all and leading to modern adherence to the rule of law.

Men like Robin Hood

Now you have imagined the days of the thirteenth century in England. Honorable men performed real deeds like those of the folk hero Robin Hood. They resisted injustice, drawing attention to excessive taxation and oppression of the people. Because of these men who fought like Robin Hood to right the wrongs of a corrupt and arbitrary rule, England began to move from royal fiat to Magna Carta to English common law. Magna Carta became the great symbol for the sovereignty of the rule of law and constitutional government in England and later for the United States Constitution.

It was past time for ending our storytelling, for it was getting late; but these true tales were as enthralling as any tale of Robin Hood, so time went quickly. Though the likes of Robin Hood who helped bring about Magna Carta were never recorded by name, their stories captivated and absorbed my schoolfellows, who were not inclined to depart. But hunger called us to dinner, and we disbanded until our next meeting for more tales of adventure.

THE END

History of the Legend

The story of Robin Hood is one of England's most famous legends, along with that of King Arthur. Its appeal is its tale of the universal desire for justice and fairness, especially in times of tyranny.

The legend of Robin Hood has been told for centuries, with written accounts dating to the 1377 poem by William Langland, "The Vision of Piers Plowman." The 1450 manuscript "Robin Hood and the Monk" rests at Cambridge University and is perhaps the oldest surviving text. Robin Hood's story was often told using ballads, which described vividly the violence of the day. Joseph Cundall (writing as "Stephen Percy") was a nineteenth-century English writer and publisher of children's books. His tale of Robin is delivered through the eyes of a schoolboy telling the story of Robin Hood to his classmates.

This version of Robin Hood is the first in a series of classic children's novels published by Hathaway House Books of Dallas, Texas. Compiled from classic versions of the tale, including Joseph Cundall's British version of 1841, Lewis and Stutts retain the high adventure of a timeless hero, expressed in rich language with vivid descriptions of Robin Hood's stories as well as historical events from the days of Robin Hood in the forests of England. Greg Ruhl's elegant illustrations captivate the heart of the reader with images that make the story come alive in a child's imagination.

Hathaway House respectfully honors those who have recorded tales of Robin Hood that have helped keep his legend alive for hundreds of years, including the tales of Stephen Percy (the penname of Joseph Cundall), Olive Beaupré Miller, Sara Hawks Sterling, George Cockburn Harvey, Hamilton Wright Mabie, and anonymous writers. We believe that worthy stories in print hold a special place in the minds and hearts of children, and we strive to present timeless tales that wholesomely feed the imagination, inspire the ambition toward greatness, and develop mature reading skills.

ROBIN R. LEWIS is the founder of Providence Christian School of Texas and the co-founder of West Dallas Community School, both in Dallas, Texas. She is a graduate of the University of Texas at Austin where she was named Outstanding Student of the McCombs School of Business. She is devoted to enriching children's lives through classical education and the love of lifelong learning. Robin has spent her entire adult life supporting families in the joy of raising children. She and her husband, Michael, live in Dallas and are the parents of four children and the grandparents of five granddaughters.

JANET STUTTS has lived and worked in Texas, American Samoa, China, Israel, and Mississippi. A generalist at heart, she holds a degree in teaching and advanced degrees in education, biblical studies, and science. Varied interests such as travel, photography, writing, music, camping, teaching, and humor feed her imagination and storytelling. Her experience with students, including many years at Providence Christian School, has helped her understand and relate to diverse groups. She feels blessed by God and her family, friends, and students. Being Aunt Janet to one niece, six nephews, their wives, and one grandniece enriches her adventure-filled life.

GREG RUHL's talent and joy for drawing was an ever-present calling growing up in Canada's small town of Hanover, Ontario. The Ontario College of Art is where he discovered illustration and, upon graduating with honors in 1981, eagerly pursued a freelance illustration career based in Toronto. His traditional painterly illustrations have garnered numerous industry awards for publishing and advertising projects. His richly engaging illustrations add an elegant dimension to this timeless tale. He was delighted to be commissioned for this work saying, "These classic books are such an ideal match to my skills and desires as an illustrator."

MISSION STATEMENT OF HATHAWAY HOUSE, LTD.

Hathaway House, Ltd. is a purveyor of fine quality books, toys, games, and educational curricula for children. To that end and with deeply held conviction:

We desire to support families in the heartfelt joy of raising children.

We believe there is no compromise in the quest to bring beauty, both visually and in language, to children to augment in them a discriminating eye and a broadening voice.

We adhere to the premise that every literary and artistic element merits attention, and we seek to employ beautiful and expansive language and wholesome images to invite children into a world of wonderment and imagination.

We will publish time-honored tales, which promote noble character, increasing discernment, and lasting understanding in the child.